A PROUD LADY

by

Helen Cannam

Dales Large Print Books
Long Preston, North Yorkshire,
BD23 4ND, England.

British Library Cataloguing in Publication Data.

Cannam, Helen
    A proud lady.

    A catalogue record of this book is
    available from the British Library

    ISBN   978-1-84262-726-6 pbk

First published in Great Britain in 1984 by Robert Hale Ltd.
under the title *The Corsair* and pseudonym *Mary Corrigan*

Copyright ©1984, 2001 by Helen Cannam
Author's Note © 2001 by Helen Cannam

Cover illustration © Len Thurston by arrangement with
P.W.A International Ltd.

Published in Large Print 2009 by arrangement with
Helen Cannam, care of Sheil Land Associates Ltd.

Dales Large Print is an imprint of Library Magna Books Ltd.

Printed and bound in Great Britain by
T.J. (International) Ltd., Cornwall, PL28 8RW

Author's Note

I welcome the return to print of this early novel of mine, though the young mother who wrote it, scribbling away after the children were in bed, seems very far removed from the person – and writer – I am now.

First published under a pen-name in the early 1980s, it was, in a sense, an apprentice work. But it was great fun to do, and I shall never forget the delight of seeing my own words in print for the first time. I hope it is still able to give pleasure to those who read it.

One

The *Proud Lady* was two days out of Portsmouth, bound for Kinsale with a cargo of luxury goods and six passengers. The evening sun, lighting the sky with rose and gold, gilded her wind-filled sails, and the scrubbed boards of her small deck, and brightened Kate Pendleton's untidy brown curls as she leaned over the rail and smiled with delight at the spray splashing into her face from the green gold waves which echoed the colour of her eyes.

Supper was over, and in the tiny stuffy cabin below Aunt Tabby was asleep at last, her misery temporarily obliterated; and Kate was released to wander on the upper deck and enjoy these last hours of freedom. She was a kind-hearted girl, and not one to rejoice at another's misfortune; and she was fond of Aunt Tabby, in an exasperated way. Even so, she could not help but be grateful for the deep sea swell which had confined her elderly relative, groaning piteously, to her bunk from the moment they left port.

Poor Aunt Tabby had such dispiriting ideas as to what constituted respectable behaviour; and wandering on deck, talking to the sailors and asking innumerable questions about the workings of the ship and the details of the voyage would, Kate knew, very definitely not have accorded with them. As it was, there was little she could do for Aunt Tabby, who for the most part wanted simply to be left alone, and Kate had enjoyed almost every moment of the journey. Tonight, as usual, she would not go to bed until the last possible moment, when she was so tired that she would sleep the instant her head touched the hard little pillow of her bunk.

She could almost imagine she was alone on board as she stood here, swept by the wind and gazing into the setting sun. For once the bustle of ship-board life was stilled, the sailors relaxed and quiet, as if moved as much as she was by the beauty of the June evening. She closed her eyes, hearing the creak of rope and canvas and timber, the ceaseless sounds of wind and waves which had become part of her life during these last lovely days. She smiled to herself in pure delight.

'I wish,' she thought rapturously, 'I could stay here for ever.'

So happy was she that when a voice broke in on her tranquillity she did not resent it as an intrusion: after all, first mate Sam Hobbs had already become her friend.

'Grand evening, Miss Pendleton. Wind set fair and a quiet sea. We should make it on the morning tide.'

In a moment her spirits had plummeted to some forgotten depth. Sam's cheerful grin as she turned to face him seemed singularly out of place. But she managed even so to return the smile.

'Are you not sorry when a voyage is over?' she asked, determinedly switching her attention away from her own feelings. She did not want to spoil today by thinking of tomorrow.

'It'll not be over for me,' he reminded her. 'There'll be the trip home, and another after that. But maybe I'm always a mite sorry when a voyage is done. Sorry; and glad too that we've made it without trouble.'

'Fair weather, and no sickness?'

'And no pirates neither.'

Kate glanced at him with renewed interest.

'Pirates?'

He nodded.

'Yes, miss. That's our worst trouble. It's

been like that the last four years, ever since 1692 when we gave the French navy a drubbing at La Hogue. With no navy left worth the mention, King Louis's put all his weight behind the privateers – they sail in his name, and bold as brass they are too. Dunkirk, Brest, St Malo – they all have their nest of corsairs, and all the little ports in between too. We lost three ships on this route just last week, to Captain Tristan de Plouvinel – he's out of St Malo, and one of the worst, believe me. No, I'll be glad that way when we're safe in Kinsale harbour – though we should be well clear of trouble by now.

Kate gave a little shiver, which had in it an element of pleasurable excitement. On the whole, though, she was glad she had not known of the danger until now, when it was past. Adventure was all very well, and life contained little enough of it; but there were limits. The next moment she was reminded that for her, very soon, excitement of any kind was likely to become a thing of the past.

'You're to be wed in Ireland then, miss? You'll be looking forward to getting there yourself.'

Gloom settled over her spirits again. Yes,

she would indeed be wed in Ireland, to handsome, wealthy Mr William Harwood, whose large Irish estates adjoined her uncle's. She had met him several times, and she knew he was kind and considerate and he cared for her. He would make her the most devoted of husbands. She ought to be very happy – especially, as Aunt Tabby had been only too ready to remind her, before seasickness deprived her of speech, in view of her past history. In these days when William of Orange was firmly established as King of England it did not do to be tainted with Jacobite loyalties, if only by association. Even so, Kate thought with regret of her disreputable past, in the company of her feckless but beloved father – now dead – and her elder brother Harry, who had disappeared years ago in the wake of the exiled King James II, for whom her father had professed a theoretical but faint-hearted loyalty. There had never been enough money, and much of the time had been spent in moving from place to place to evade a continuous stream of creditors, but it had been fun. For all its orderliness and comfort, life with Aunt Tabby and her friends was never fun. It was, of course, to escape finally from that disreputable past that her respectable relations had

15

arranged this desirable marriage for her; and she could think of no good reason to object to it. She was single, homeless, and not at all beautiful; and her only fortune was a dowry left to her by her grandfather. She was very lucky indeed to have such a bright prospect before her.

She realised suddenly that Sam Hobbs was watching her with interest, intrigued by the long silence which had followed his question. She smiled, colouring a little.

'Yes, I'll be wed soon,' she said at last, and hurriedly began to question him about past voyages he had made, a subject dear to his heart on which he would talk for hours, if encouraged.

This time was no exception, and Kate listened enthralled as he told her of storms and shipwrecks and dangerous tropical seas, and the amazing and incredible wonders he had seen on shore. She did not quite believe every word of it, but it made very enjoyable listening.

Her attention had not wandered exactly; but it was half way through a dramatic account of a disastrous voyage to the West Indies that Kate changed her position slightly and saw a small black dot on the horizon. She rubbed her eyes, and looked again, and decided it was some kind of ship, a very long way off. She could not see at this distance if it was moving at all.

Aware of her sudden preoccupation Sam paused and turned to follow her gaze.

'It's a ship, isn't it?' she asked.

'Aye,' said Sam slowly. 'Aye, it's a ship.' And he stood quite still, eyes narrowed and hand raised to shade them, staring at the tiny speck. There was something in his stillness, something frozen almost, which set Kate's scalp prickling.

'What is it?' she asked sharply. He turned to look at her, and smiled very briefly, and shrugged.

'A ship,' was all he said.

The next moment there was a shouted order from the Captain and a sudden bustle of activity over the deck. Sam glanced at Kate again, murmured, 'We've full sail already,' and left her to ponder the significance of that cryptic remark. She saw him a little later, very occupied with some task in the prow of the ship, his talk with her clearly completely forgotten.

Kate stood for some time watching the sailors at work, fascinated as always by their agility as they scrambled up the rigging, by the skill which told them exactly how to adjust a rope or a sail to catch the full force of the wind. She felt the ship move forward with a renewed surge of speed. And then she turned to glance over her shoulder at the speck on the horizon.

It was no longer a speck, nor by now was it on the horizon. It was still a long way off, but in that short time it had come swiftly nearer to the *Proud Lady*, near enough for the setting sun to turn its wide sails to molten gold, and light up its grandeur, and its size, and its graceful lines. Even Kate in her ignorance could see that it was built for speed as well as strength.

There was a new urgency now in the activity on board the *Proud Lady*. The tension reached her, as tangible as a rope stretched to breaking point. There was no singing, and no talk; nothing but anxious eyes glancing at the following ship, and the patter of hard-soled feet on the deck. She knew, instinctively, that the little merchant ship was moving with all the speed she could muster. There was no more they could do.

For some reason Kate was not afraid. It was almost as if she was watching a drama in which she had no part, but was simply an interested spectator, unaffected by what was happening before her eyes. She turned her head from time to time to look at the ship, quickly gaining on them now, almost ready to admire its splendour, though her mind knew it brought deadly danger. When a sailor shouted 'It's the *Marguerite!*' she only wondered with interest what that meant to him.

The *Marguerite* was near enough soon to tower over the little merchantman, a great menacing bird, sails spread like wings, ready to fall on its prey. Kate stood gazing at the gilded prow, the carved figurehead, the little swarming figures on its decks. And then a shot rang out, and a great ragged hole rent the *Proud Lady's* main sail. And only then did Kate run for the greater shelter of the lower deck below the forecastle.

There was a sudden terrible shuddering crash, and the deck slid wildly beneath her. She clung to the rail of the companionway, holding tight until the ship righted itself. And then under a spattering hail of shots they boarded her.

Kate stood transfixed, as if her limbs had lost all power to move, watching in helpless disbelief as wild uncouth men swarmed like ants over the ship, swords and knives gleaming evilly in their hands.

'It's not happening – it's not real,' said a

little voice in her head. It was like a dream, something from which she knew she would wake in a moment or two. As in a dream it all happened with a horrible inevitability, a frightening speed. There was no resistance – that would have been suicidal, from un-armed sailors faced with an attack from such a large force, armed to the teeth. In what seemed like no time at all the decks were cleared of all the familiar faces, and only strangers were left.

Strangers who now had time for her.

Too late, she turned to run below deck – and found her arm grabbed from behind.

'No!' She struggled wildly, hardly knowing that it was she who had screamed. There would have been no safety below now any-way, for they were pushing past her to drag out the passengers and the remaining crew. She heard shouts and screams. 'Aunt Tabby!' she murmured in dismay, and the hand tightened its grasp painfully on her arm. She turned her head to find herself looking into a dark face beneath a shock of red hair, and a grinning mouth full of bad teeth. She shivered; but still she could not believe it was real, that she was in any danger. She was Kate Pendleton, going to Ireland to be married. Things like this did not happen to her.

Another man grasped her other arm and she was dragged with them towards the stern. Surely she must wake soon, to hear Aunt Tabby groaning in the bunk below, and the sailors changing duties over her head?

But there was no awakening yet. The men grouped in the stern were strangers, armed and hostile, and among them one towering over the rest, a great black-haired giant of a man in a scarlet coat, gold embroidered, whose black eyes ran bright and menacing over her as her captors brought her before him.

He merely gave a careless wave of a long brown hand cuffed in ruffed lace, and they shoved her to one side, to stand with the silent huddled crewmen of the *Proud Lady*.

One by one the other passengers were brought to join them. Aunt Tabby was white and weeping, her seasickness driven out by fear. Kate put a comforting arm about her, and for the first time began to think: 'This is real. It is happening to all of us, here and now.' Yet even so she had the odd feeling that she was trying to convince herself, as if to prepare herself for whatever was to come. She turned to look at the tall man who gave the orders, and shivered. She was sure they could expect no mercy from him.

'Miss Pendleton,' came a quiet voice behind her. She turned her head to see one of her fellow passengers, a merchant from Portsmouth. 'Miss Pendleton, did I not hear you say you spoke French? These are French pirates, I believe. Perhaps you would speak for us all.'

Kate glanced at the pirate Captain again, and swallowed.

'I'm not sure that he'll be interested in talking.'

'We're Englishmen,' said Mr Porter indignantly, but still in an undertone. 'And this is an English ship. They must let us go.'

'Ferme ta gueule!' commanded a man nearby, shoving at Kate. It was not a polite request for silence, and anger flared in her.

'Je peux parler français,' she retorted bravely, speaking distinctly, if with a marked terror. 'Je parlerai pour tous.' She hoped she was indeed saying that she wished to speak for everyone. Her schoolroom French was not always reliable. She had a sudden horrible fear that their safety might depend upon its accuracy, and felt very sick.

The gigantic Captain took one step towards her and stood looking down at her from his great height, mockery in his grin.

'And I,' he said, in a voice as powerful as his whole presence, 'I, Tristan de Plouvinel, speak English. We are in any case not French, mademoiselle, but Breton. We have no need of your services.' Then, horribly, he tilted his head to one side and the grin broadened, dazzlingly white. 'Or have we, perhaps?'

Kate felt herself go very cold. Pirates raped captive women, so they said. Was that what he had in mind? She edged away from him; and then to her astonishment found that Aunt Tabby, tiny and trembling, had pushed forward to stand in front of her.

'You leave my niece alone, you scoundrel! She's a virtuous girl, and betrothed to Mr William Harwood, of whom even you may have heard – a man of wealth and position and influence in high places. Lay one finger on her, and it will be the worse for you.'

Too late, Kate realised what her aunt in her ignorance had done. She reached out a hand to restrain her, just as the Captain raised an interested black eyebrow and said: 'Indeed? We must talk more of this.' He gestured to two of his men, and gave a command in French so colloquial that Kate could not understand it.

The next moment she found herself being marched away from the others across the deck to where the rope-ladder of the *Marguerite* swung just within reach to take her swaying and trembling on to the pirate ship. There she was marched across a vast deck lined with polished guns, down a steep ladder and into a narrow hold, to a small dark room; and locked firmly in, alone.

Two

In all her short disorderly life Kate had never lived through a night so dreadful as the one that faced her now. When she first heard the bolt pushed sharply into place behind her, it was already too dark for her to make out any details of the room where she was confined. Even when her eyes grew more accustomed to the dimness she could make out only the faint outline of a tiny window, a square of grey-green spattered with spray, moving now and then so that it caught a last faint gleam of dying sunlight. All she could discover, by hesitant touch, was that the room was small and bare and contained a low hard bunk upon which she placed herself with caution. From beyond the door sounds reached her of wind in the rigging, and much further off the shouts of sailors.

She wondered with a sickening chill what was happening to her fellow prisoners. What, above all, of Aunt Tabby? She had unwittingly presented Captain de Plouvinel with a prize, disclosing that Kate offered the possibility of a rich ransom. Kate wondered now if that would really make her position worse, or if instead Aunt Tabby's indiscretion might have saved her life – or at least her virtue. But if that was so, what did it mean for the other passengers, who had no such protection? And what did it mean for poor dear nervous Aunt Tabby, with whom the Captain had promised to 'talk more'? Kate could imagine only too well what form that talk might take.

She wished now, in fact, that her imagination was not so vivid, that she did not have the quick intuitive intelligence she had inherited from her long-dead mother. It would certainly be better now to sit here, a prisoner, without the least idea what was going to happen, fearing the unknown, rather than dreaming up a limitless number of possibilities. All the pirate tales she had ever heard – and until now she had not known she had heard so many – came back to her through the long hours of that interminable night in all their full and lurid detail. She longed to sleep, but when she did doze at last it was only to be plunged into dreams so appalling that she forced herself to wake again. From the moment the pirates had boarded the *Proud Lady* it had seemed as if she was living in a nightmare; but the world of actual nightmare was even worse, though that scarcely seemed possible.

At some stage during the night, when it was at last fully dark, there was a sudden surge of movement beyond the locked door. Shouts, running feet, the bustle of a ship's crew at work reached her, close at hand; and at last the ship began slowly, steadily, to get under way, rolling over the sea towards some unknown destination. What had become of the *Proud Lady*, and her crew, and her passengers? Had she been scuttled, and sunk to the bottom of the sea; and the prisoners with her? Kate shivered, and prayed that some miracle had preserved the others unhurt. But she was not very hopeful. She wondered if she would ever see Aunt Tabby again.

She was glad when dawn came at last, a faint grey light creeping into the little room, disclosing that it was as bare and comfortless as she had imagined: the darkness had not hidden anything. She felt by now cold and cramped and stiff-limbed. She had not lain down on the hard bunk, but sat all night huddled in fear on the edge, as if she might somehow be safer that way. Since there was not even a blanket on the wooden slats she would in any case have found little rest on

27

its unyielding surface.

She hoped that now it was light someone might come. She had reached the point where she felt she would welcome any company, just so long as she was no longer alone. Once or twice she heard steps close at hand, and straightened herself to face the opening of the door; but it remained firmly closed. She began to feel a new and quieter misery, and shed a few slow tears. They brought no relief, though, and there seemed little point in weeping when there was no one to see and certainly no one to comfort her.

Much later she found herself slumped forward with her head on her knees and realised she had been asleep, deeply and without dreaming. She felt just a little better for it, and somewhat less fearful as to what might happen to her. Perhaps after all her fate as a hostage might be a more desirable one than that of the other prisoners. But she wished she knew what had happened to Aunt Tabby.

At last – about mid-morning, judging by the strength of the sunlight on the waves beyond her window – the approaching steps did come to a halt outside, and the door opened, and a villainous-looking man came in, bringing with him a strong and wholly unpleasant aroma of sweat and dirt mingled with garlic. She shrank back, suddenly afraid again. But he did no more than hold out to her a couple of dry biscuits and a tankard. After a moment's hesitation, she took them, and he left her almost at once, without saying anything. She heard the bolt slam into place again.

The biscuits were not very appetising, but better than nothing; the tankard contained wine of dubious quality, which she drank without enthusiasm, because she did not want to feel faint if she had to face some new and unexpected ordeal. But for several hours afterwards she was left undisturbed, as the heat grew, and the ship rolled on. She passed the time by pacing the floor of the little cabin; gazing out of the window at the rising and falling green-blue of the waves, and the cloudless blue of the sky above, finding some kind of entertainment in the occasional passing flight of a gull; and waiting.

Eventually, she supposed, they would reach a port. Or at least she assumed a prisoner for ransom would be likely to be held somewhere on shore. She tried not to imagine under what conditions she might be imprisoned; or what would happen if William could not, or would not, pay whatever ransom was demanded. She toyed briefly with the possibility that her betrothed, a man of some past military experience, would come in person to her rescue; but she knew almost at once that such a dramatic – and doomed – gesture would be quite out of character. No one could ever have accused William of recklessness.

It must have been well into the afternoon when the cabin door opened again and a man – the same as before, or another, she could not be sure – grasped her arm and made it clear she was to come with him. He said something, too, but she was too frightened to take it in. She had in any case no thought of arguing with him. Hobbling a little at first, for the small space of her cabin did not allow much relief for cramped limbs, she went where he dragged her, none too gently, screwing up her eyes against the sudden brightness of the sunlight.

A quick glance as they crossed the deck showed her there was still no sign of land; and that her fellow passengers from the *Proud Lady* were nowhere to be seen. The next moment her guard led her down a companion-way to a long lower gun-deck where he halted at last before a handsome oak door, and knocked briskly upon it. At a shout from inside he opened it, and pushed her in ahead of him. She found herself in a large airy cabin, luxuriously furnished; and standing face to face with Captain de Plouvinel.

He sat at his ease in a cushioned tasselled armchair at the far side of a wide table which yet looked too small for his great height. His long legs were stretched beneath it, his arms spread across its surface. And his black eyes were watching her intently from beneath the heavy dark brows.

He gave a wave of one hand, dismissing her companion; and then rose with a slow grace which was a little surprising in someone so tall, and pulled a chair forward, closer to the table, for Kate to sit on. It was a moment or two before she realised what he intended, and she took her seat at last in some confusion. She found the intent scrutiny of those black eyes more than a little disquieting.

She had no intention, however, of letting him see that she was uncomfortable or afraid. She sat very straight, her hands folded quietly in her lap, and waited, her eyes on his face, to hear why he had summoned her.

There was a moment or two of silence, during which she noticed the strong dark lines of his face: the long nose and firm jaw, the straight brows, the unexpectedly supple mouth. It was odd how very aware she was of the breadth of his shoulders, the length of his body and the fine strong legs, the sensitive power of his hands. He was broad, yet lean; strong, powerful; yet graceful in movement. It was an intriguing combination. In spite of her fear, in spite of her helpless position, Kate found herself wondering about him, curious as to what kind of man he was, or what had made him take up his cruel trade. She had not until now thought of pirates as human beings, with strengths and weaknesses like herself, or her brother Harry; or Aunt Tabby.

Aunt Tabby–! All else forgotten, the question broke sharply from her. 'What have you done with my aunt?'

Tristan de Plouvinel leaned comfortably back in his chair as if he had not a care in the world. The gesture stirred a little surge of anger to life in Kate; which was startled into quiescence as soon as he spoke. She had heard his voice last night, of course, but she had forgotten how deep it was, and how resonant, its tones vibrating through her in a way which was both strange and deeply disturbing.

'Your aunt was most helpful, mademoiselle. She goes home, very soon.'

Kate stared at him, wondering if she could believe him. Or did the words imply something else, something sinister, something too terrible to be spoken aloud?

'What do you mean?' she asked quickly. He smiled, clearly amused by her suspicion.

'Exactly that. She and the others of that ship are already on their way to Ireland. Your aunt, of course, bears a letter for that important man, your betrothed. Let us hope he will be sensible of your needs.'

Kate felt some of the colour drain from her face.

'What...' she asked, with some difficulty, for her mouth was dry, 'what will happen if ... if he isn't?'

The Captain shrugged and spread his fine hands.

'Who can say? Let us not think of it. Meanwhile, you are my guest, and what I have is at your disposal—'

'How generous!' Kate broke in with asperity. He merely smiled cheerfully: it was a boyish and oddly attractive smile, lightening the dark face. Kate felt her stomach give a lurch, and knew it was not from fear. This giant of a man had an uncomfortable effect on her, quite apart from the threat he posed.

Yet she knew she had every reason to be afraid of him.

'Of course, you may not go free – but in other respects, I hope your stay will be as comfortable as possible.'

Just as if he was mine host of some superior inn, thought Kate angrily. She burst out: 'Stop playing games – I am your prisoner. How can you pretend otherwise?'

'I seek only to make it as easy as I can for you,' he returned, quite unruffled. 'I am not a cruel man. If you cooperate with me, then all will be well – so long, of course, as the ransom is paid also.'

'Otherwise, I suppose,' said Kate in a tone whose acidity countered a rapidly beating heart, 'you will be forced against your better nature to behave like – shall we say? – a pirate?'

He grinned again, his eyes sparkling with amusement.

'I should deplore that most deeply, mademoiselle,' he replied with a deprecatory gesture of his fluent hands. 'And of course I am not a pirate – I abhor the term, and reject it absolutely.'

'Oh?' returned Kate. 'Then I imagined what happened last night, I suppose. Or is boarding unarmed merchant ships a part of legitimate warfare these days?'

'Our countries *are* at war, Miss Pendleton. And I serve the interests of France. I am a corsair, mademoiselle, armed with my King's authority.'

'I don't suppose your victims appreciate the distinction,' retorted Kate. 'Certainly I do not.'

'Then you ought. For were I a pirate, I fear I should treat you with rather less than courtesy.' He rose to his feet, his great height seeming at once to dominate the spacious cabin. 'As it is, I shall now escort you to your new quarters, where you will remain until we reach St Malo in the morning.'

'Why don't you just say "I'll take you to your prison"? Fine words don't make it any better.'

'You talk too much, Miss Pendleton. Mere prisoners do not waste their breath in argument.'

'I hadn't noticed you were lost for words either.'

He laughed briefly, and held out his arm to her. She gazed at him blankly for a moment, and then realised he meant her to take hold of it, for all the world as if he were a gentleman leading his partner in to supper. Kate felt inclined to refuse him, with some sharp

35

retort; but he caught her eye and there was something in his expression which warned her to be careful. 'For all the fine words,' it said, 'you are my prisoner. I have power of life and death over you. You would do well to be careful.'

Coldly, with a gesture which was distantly correct, but no more, she laid her hand on his arm and he led her to the door.

As they crossed the gun deck, Kate wondered what would happen if she were to remove her hand from his arm and run from him: there was no one else about. But there was no point at all in making such an attempt. Where after all could she go, but into the sea? And she could not swim. However unpleasant her situation, she had no wish to drown. She sensed too that her fate at the hands of Captain de Plouvinel's sailors might be less than pleasant, if he were not around to ensure her safety. No, she was on the whole better off in the Captain's company, however unwelcome.

He had, she realised soon, not exaggerated when he described her new prison as offering 'comfortable seclusion'. Nothing could have contrasted more with the tiny bare room of last night than did the panelled well-lit cabin to which he took her now, richly furnished, the wide bunk spread, over visibly comfortable bedding, with an embroidered coverlet, the windows curtained, and even a glowing red Turkey carpet lying on the floor. In spite of herself, she paused momentarily in the doorway to draw breath with astonishment. She was annoyed with herself for doing so, however, for her companion paused too, and looked at her with a faint smile of exasperating smugness upon his face. His expression said in the clearest terms: 'I told you so.'

'I think,' he said, still smiling, 'without fear of contradiction, that you will pass the time here not without comfort until we reach port. Your meals will be served to you there.' He gestured towards a polished table, at which stood a carved chair. Then he turned, and before she could draw back had taken her hand in his. 'Now, mademoiselle, I leave you. But if you lack anything you have only to speak to the man who stands beyond your door, and your needs will be supplied. I bid you good-day.' The next moment he had bent his dark head and placed a light kiss upon her hand; and then he left her.

Kate stood quite still for a long time staring at the closed door, her eyes wide and wondering. Then, slowly, she raised her hand

and looked at it, as if half expecting to find some tainting mark upon it where his lips had touched it. But there was nothing, though she could still feel the faint, firm pressure, the cool smoothness of that kiss. She was trembling a little now, from reaction she supposed. She drew a deep breath, and crossed to the long mirror set against the far wall, and studied her dishevelled appearance. She must try and restore it to some kind of order.

'I don't know why I thought my virtue was in danger,' she said to herself. 'Looking like this is enough to frighten anyone away.' Even with hair and gown tidied, and the dust washed from face and hands, her appearance was, she felt, little more encouraging. She made a critical study of the too prominent front teeth – not improved by the gap between them – the freckles lightly dusting a nose which was too short and too tilted at the tip for beauty, the slight slender figure lacking any hint of the voluptuous curves essential to a lady of fashion. 'I don't think I would pay anyone a ransom to rescue me,' she thought dejectedly. But almost at once she told herself not to think of such things. William had asked her to marry him; she must mean something to him. Surely then he would pay what was asked to have her restored to be his bride? She must convince herself that it was only a matter of time, and meanwhile make the best of this irksome period of captivity. She would not allow herself to recognise that if Aunt Tabby had not spoken out on her behalf she might well by now be on her way home with the others. It would not help if she allowed any bitterness to taint her mood.

At least, she told herself bracingly, it began to look as if she would be treated with courtesy. She could even try to look upon it as an adventure, an exciting event with which she could entertain family and friends for years to come. The thought gave her courage, and when supper came – simple food, but carefully prepared – she was even able to eat it with enjoyment.

Calmed by her resolution, she slept well that night.

Three

They were within sight of land. Kate could hear the delighted shouts of the sailors, the increased activity on the deck above her head, the raucous deafening cries of the gulls wheeling in search of scraps dropped by the *Marguerite*. She abandoned her half-eaten breakfast and ran to the window – a wide, handsome window running across the whole stern of the ship, like that in a house. But for all its width she could see nothing apart from the inevitable stretch of blue sea and blue sky, and the white-flecked wake left by the ship in the clear water.

After a few minutes of fruitless gazing out of the window, she stood up and began to pace the cabin. The sounds told her unmistakably that they were close to land, and the Captain had said they would reach St Malo in the morning. It was unbearably frustrating to be able to see nothing at all. She wished that someone would come for her.

What was it like, she wondered: this notorious nest of pirates, this hostile city which was to be her prison? Even in the adventurous days in her father's company she had never been so far from home as this – never, indeed, imagined that she would ever find herself in the strange, lonely, desperate situation which faced her now. She had, though, enough of her father's stubborn optimism to face the future with courage, and a determination that it should not destroy her spirit.

After a time she went back to the window again, and now at last there was something to see. A succession of rocky islands, dark and rugged, slid by; one crowned with a fort that looked as if it had grown from the rock itself. Distantly a low dark line rimmed the horizon, marking the point where the land began: the land of France, England's ancient enemy, and the refuge now of the luckless King James. With a sudden quickening heartbeat, Kate thought: 'Harry followed King James into exile – perhaps he too is in France.' But common sense reminded her at once that France was a large country, and St Malo, as far as she could remember, a very long way from the exiled court at St Germain-en-Laye. And she, Kate Pendleton, was a lonely and helpless prisoner. Even so, it did cheer her a little to think that she was, perhaps, just a little nearer to her beloved brother.

The ship must have altered course slightly, for the land had disappeared again. Kate returned to the table and finished her breakfast, reminding herself sensibly that she might need all her strength later. After all, in this new unpredictable situation regular meals and any kind of routine were unlikely, she suspected, to play much part.

There were new sounds now outside. More shouting, far off as well as near; clattering and hammering; the rattle of wheels on cobbles, and the running of feet. The *Marguerite* was almost motionless, rocking gently on the slight waves of some sheltered harbour. Slowly, shutting out the light, a high gaunt granite wall came relentlessly into view, dark and forbidding. Above it, just visible, were the close crowded roofs of a city.

Kate shivered. She began to understand what it might mean to be a prisoner in this place, not with dancing waves to watch from a wide window, but shut in by dark walls, without light or air or sunshine. The sense of adventure which had sustained her until now abruptly left her. She drew several deep breaths to calm the sudden trembling of her limbs. When they came for her, as they surely would very soon, they must not know how frightened she was.

When two of the crew did come for her, entering unceremoniously without a knock, they found her standing quietly by the window, hands folded before her (it was easier to keep them still that way), clear eyes watching them steadily as they approached. Though she did not understand all they said to her, the meaning was plain enough, and she did not wait for them to lay hands on her before stepping forward, ready to go with them. They led her at a brisk pace to the upper deck, and from there at last she had a clear view of her destination.

The *Marguerite* lay at anchor in a wide bay, guarded at its farthest point by a rocky, tree-grown headland, and here, near at hand, by the rampart-encircled city. A long spit of sand and rock linked the city to the inner curve of the bay, but Kate could see that at high tide the water would cover that part completely, turning St Malo into an island, defended from all its enemies by the natural aids of rock and wave. And making it impossible for anyone to enter or leave without a boat. She turned to gaze more intently at the city, her nostrils assailed by an unfamiliar mixture of smells: pitch, and fish, and the pungent odours of the armaments factories from which the citizens supplied the corsairs on whom their prosperity depended. That the city was prospering was clear. At one side, commanding a fine view of sea and bay alike, and of all the ships coming and going between the two, the masons had clearly been hard at work for some hours already in the clear morning light, building fine new houses in the implacable granite of the surrounding city, houses fit only for men of wealth and position.

Closer to the harbour the crowded roofs and the intensity of the smells and noises told her that here the working men lived: the shipwrights and fishmongers, the gunsmiths and tavernkeepers, and all the other tradespeople and craftsmen on whom the corsairs depended. Beyond the roofs, the high bell tower of a great church – the cathedral, she was later to learn – rose impressively, echoed faintly by the spires of lesser churches dotted here and there among the roofs.

Close at hand, towering over the yards of the shipbuilders and the quay where sailors and townsfolk and women crowded to welcome the *Marguerite*, rose the solid granite keep of a castle, standing guard over the city at its one weak point, where the tide left it vulnerable to approach by land. Unwillingly, Kate found her gaze drawn again and again to its threatening bulk, and wondered: 'Is that where I'll be held?'

It was a relief when a voice close behind her broke into her thoughts.

'Welcome to St Malo, mademoiselle. You will now taste the very best of the hospitality we can offer.'

She turned sharply, angered by the mocking note in the words, a note echoed in the dark eyes looking down at her. And then as her gaze met those eyes she found herself colouring deeply, and bent her head quickly to hide her confusion. It was infuriating to find herself so easily overcome when she needed so desperately to keep cool and calm. It must, she supposed, be the bright boldness of Captain de Plouvinel's dark eyes which so disturbed her. Horrible man that he was, to be so unconcerned for her feelings! Perhaps it would even be a relief to find herself incarcerated in some solitary prison well away from his discomforting presence. Yet even there, something told her, she would not be free of him. She had her head bent now, and she knew he had turned away from her to give his attention to some other matter, yet she felt his presence still, aware as clearly as if she saw it of the strong powerful lines of his body, the sense of animal alert-

45

ness allied to animal grace, like that of some great wild jungle cat. He had not touched her, yet she felt again that curious vibration running through her which had struck her when he bent last night to kiss her hand.

He had already put her to the back of his mind, she realised that almost immediately. She heard him call out an order in that deeply disturbing voice, and then he strode away from her, his brown hands gesturing to emphasise the force of his words. A little later, a small boat was lowered on to the water, and she was urged into it by her escort and rowed to the quay.

It was a shock to find herself suddenly transported to the heart of the milling throng below the high city walls. From the ship, looking down on them, the crowd had not seemed so dense, nor the noise, lessened by distance, so great. Now it was all about her, clamorous and bewildering. She was jostled and pushed, her gown caught by dragging hands, the hood of her cloak brushed from her head. She was even glad of the hands on either side holding her firmly as they steered her through the crowd to the Grande Porte of the city, the impressive main gate over which *Notre Dame de Secours*, the painted and flower-decked statue of the Virgin, kept a benign watch on the narrow, stinking, crowded streets, echoing with a babble of chaotic sound.

At a brisk pace her escorts led her through one street, and another, on as if in a maze, up steps and down, this way and that, until they came to a halt at last in a narrow alley a little quieter than the rest, before a high-gabled, stone-based, wooden-framed house which gave the impression of being all glass, so wide and numerous were its windows. Here, the men hammered on the door, and after a brief exchange with the servant who opened it, led her inside.

The room in which she found herself now was wide and spacious and filled the whole ground floor of the house. There were windows on all sides, from the low-beamed ceiling to the cushioned window seats, and even on either side of the granite fireplace, a feature as solid and durable in appearance as the city walls. The floor was carpeted, the windows hung with curtains, and the furniture was at once heavy and luxurious. On one side, facing the fireplace, the inevitable windows looked on to a tiny lush garden, partly enclosed by neighbouring houses, and shut off from the street by a high wall.

After a further discussion between her

escort and the man who had admitted them, she was led to a door which opened to reveal two flights of stairs, one descending to some hidden depths, the other leading to the floor above. There, now, she was taken, across a small half-landing and on up to the second floor high under the roof. She was admitted to a small room at the rear of the house, simply but adequately furnished, whose wide windows gave, beyond the crowding roofs and chimneys, a brief glittering view of the sea. She had just time to take in the realisation that her prison was not after all to be the grim lightless dungeon she had imagined before the men left her, locking the door firmly behind them.

In sudden trembling reaction, Kate sank down on the low bed and closed her eyes. From a great distance the noises of the city reached her, and underlying them the soft whisper of waves on the shore beyond the ramparts. Closer at hand, from somewhere in the house below the room where she lay, she could hear the clatter of pots and a snatch of song sung in a cheerful unmusical female voice. So she was not the only woman under this roof! She was astonished at the sense of relief that gave her, as if in some way it made her less alone, less helpless.

Marie Ange herself made a noisy entrance to the little room after the English girl had been there for about half an hour. She was a round rosy-cheeked young woman, with bright dark eyes and a friendly manner, and she came to inform Kate that she had been ordered by Captain de Plouvinel to offer any help that might be needed by the prisoner. She did not stay long, since Kate could think of no immediate needs for the maid to satisfy; but when she had gone Kate felt greatly comforted, knowing she was somewhere in the house, within hearing distance of a shout or a cry.

It was Marie Ange who brought her a meal of broth and bread some time around midday; and a more substantial supper late in the afternoon. Otherwise Kate saw no one all day. From time to time there were sounds of activity downstairs, and once Kate thought she heard the Captain's deep tones speaking as if he were in a hurry. But she was left firmly alone. At first she was glad of the quiet, and the opportunity to rest and gather her thoughts; but after a time it became tedious in the extreme, shut in that little room with nothing at all to do but gaze at the distant sea hoping for the chance sight of a passing ship, or gulls squabbling noisily over a scrap.

At last, late in the evening, just as she was wondering whether to go to bed – though there was still about an hour of daylight left – she heard the sound of someone coming upstairs; and a moment later Marie Ange came in with one of the men who had been her escort this morning, a fair-haired man with a badly scarred face. She was, they told her, to come below, for Captain de Plouvinel wished to speak to her. And she must bring her cloak with her.

She wondered as she followed them downstairs what that might mean. Was the little room only a temporary resting place? Was she after all to be taken to the fearsome dungeon of this morning's fears? Her heart beat clamorously, and she drew her cloak close about her, as if for protection.

In the spacious living-room below the Captain was waiting.

'Ah, bien,' he said approvingly. 'You are well clad, I see. It can be cool on the ramparts at evening.'

So she was going to be taken away from here! Kate tried not to let the alarm show on her face. It was something other than alarm though which made it so hard to breathe steadily and brought the colour rushing to her face as the Captain crossed the room to her side. It was some consolation, she supposed, that he did not appear to notice her confusion. Brisk and practical, and clearly with little time to waste, he ordered her to come with him. The scarred seaman followed them at a discreet distance.

Out in the narrow street, overhung by the upper storey of the house and of others like it, the air was cooler now, fresh and salty. The sun had almost gone, and here the shadows were already long and deep, dark enough in the little alleys to conceal a man. Kate shivered, and was glad of the powerful presence of the Captain at her side. He might have a disturbing effect on her, but at least in his company she knew no other dangers could threaten her.

He was silent as he led her through the confusing network of little streets to where the city walls rose black against the pale evening sky. She ventured a glance at his face, and saw that it had a dark shuttered look, the expression of a busy man engaged on some necessary task which must be accomplished before more important matters could again engage his attention. It was perfectly obvious that whatever effect he might have on her, she interested him not at all, except as a convenient way to make money. Presumably he was eager now to ensure that she was held in some secure place from which escape was impossible.

At the wall he led her up a narrow flight of steps, past a guard who exchanged a curt greeting, and up on to the broad stone-paved summit of the ramparts. There, facing out from the city to the surrounding sea, he came to a halt. And Kate drew in her breath in wonder.

Beneath a low fiery sun the sea lay silver and rose, streaking the pale smooth sands with dazzling rivulets, for the tide was low now, and the beach stretched out from the walls to the dark rocky islets she had seen from the ship. Immediately below her the walls fell steeply, rooted in black rock; and in contrast to their rugged strength the edge of the sea, far off, was fringed with a delicate lacework of white foam, edged by the setting sun with rose. Kate stood enraptured by the wild loveliness of it all, and it was some time before she became aware that her companion was watching her.

'Beautiful, is it not?' he asked unexpectedly. But before she could agree, he went on: 'Observing all this' – He gave a sweeping gesture with one hand – 'you would think, would you not, that it would be a simple matter to walk to the mainland of our country. You saw, perhaps, that at one point to the south of here, our city is joined to the land. When the tide is low, as now, it is easily crossed. Then, you might think, one might quickly lose oneself in the countryside, and so escape. But make no mistake, mademoiselle, the appearances deceive you. The tide comes quickly in. You choose the wrong moment to cross, and you are lost, for at high tide the sea rages over that point, and the force of it is deadly. And even should you choose the right moment, there are always watchmen on guard to see that no one comes or goes that should not. You have already been seen, and noted. Try to cross, and before you take two steps they will lay hands on you.' Looking up at his dark eyes, hearing the grimly urgent note in his voice, Kate believed him, completely. 'Then, perhaps,' he went on, 'you will think: ah, but at night it is dark, and the guards cannot see. Then, if the tide is right, I can cross – or find a boat perhaps. That seems possible, mademoiselle?'

Knowing full well that in a moment or two he would demonstrate that it was nothing of the kind, Kate nodded. Agreement was clearly expected of her.

'Then,' said the Captain with marked satisfaction, 'we shall wait and you will see.'

Puzzled, Kate stood obediently beside him, silent as he was, watching the sun sink slowly into the sea and wondering what they were waiting for.

And then, a few brief moments later, she knew. First, loud and sudden above the evening sounds of the city, came the rattling clamour of a bell, insistent, imperious.

'The curfew,' the Captain told her. 'It is ten o'clock.'

Behind them, men and women called out, ran through the streets, slammed doors, shuttered windows, momentarily intensifying the din. And then, as dusk fell over shore and rock and walls, quietness settled with it, silencing the streets, but for the wail of a child, a woman shouting in anger, the distant barking of a dog. Kate directed a questioning glance at the Captain. Clearly he was still waiting.

There was not one dog barking now, but many, a whole host of dogs, somewhere to the left of where they stood, deep, harsh, frenetic barking. And then in a moment the shore below them was scattered with black running forms, and the barking filled the night air.

'The guardians of St Malo,' said the Captain. 'Our sure defence through the hours of darkness. There are twenty-four of these mastiffs, very strong and powerful, and quite untrained to any master but the one man who feeds them. And they have not eaten since dawn.' Without knowing it, Kate moved closer to her companion. He looked down at her with a wry little smile. 'So, you see, to venture outside the walls at night would be – unwise. They run free there until dawn, every night, all night, when the gates are closed. And they do not know a tender English girl from an enemy.'

Kate shuddered.

'Has ... has anyone ever...?' she broke off, too appalled by the thought to end the sentence.

'But of course, mademoiselle. There are always the careless, the rash, the unwary. Our guardians have supped often on the meat of our city's enemies. Afterwards, it is not often possible to know for certain who the unfortunate one was.' He studied her for a moment, then said: 'You are cold, I think, mademoiselle. Let us now return home. I told you, did I not, that our city would welcome you, and offer you its most generous hospitality? In my house, amongst my servants, that will indeed be true. Try to escape, and the hospitality will be of a different kind.'

Kate nodded dumbly, and could think of nothing further to say as he led her back through the now deserted streets to the house of many windows. A little later, she heard the key turn in the lock of her room with an enormous sense of relief. 'No,' she thought: 'You need have no fear, Captain de Plouvinel. I shall not try to escape.' It took her some time that night to banish from her mind the memory of those dark panting shapes on the rocks, and her mental picture of what they might do to her if she were to venture beyond the walls. She was glad at least that her sleep, if fitful, was untroubled by nightmares.

She was astonished to find that her first sensation on waking next morning was one of excitement. It seemed such an inappropriate reaction for someone in her unpleasant position. Yet now that she was sure of her physical safety she felt that she had no need for fear, unless she tried to escape. And in some strange way she felt that the prospect of passing her captivity in the company of Captain de Plouvinel was a good deal more entertaining than going meekly on to Ireland and her respectable marriage.

After all, she told herself as she dressed, not every girl is able to say she has been taken prisoner by St Malo corsairs. It was only fitting that she should make the most of it.

Then Marie Ange came with her breakfast, and stayed to talk a little, and told her that the *Marguerite* would sail tomorrow on a fresh voyage, and Captain de Plouvinel with her. Disappointment struck Kate like a blow. There would surely be little prospect of excitement in a captivity spent in comfortable seclusion, without good company. Perhaps though, she thought hopefully, the Captain would at least send for her, to give her some final instructions as to how she must behave. All through the long slow day she heard every step on the stair with a tremor of lively anticipation. But the Captain neither came, nor sent for her, and the hours passed, and night fell again. And then she knew it was too late. He had done all that was needed when he warned her against trying to escape, and now he had put her out of his mind.

She stood at the window next morning, and watched the ships disappear over the horizon, and wondered if any of them carried her captor, and was astonished at the depth of the despondency which settled over her spirits now that she knew that he had gone.

Four

Captain de Plouvinel had after all thought once more of Kate before he left. He had put aside a handful of books for her, with apologies that none of them were in English, and Marie Ange had instructions to provide the prisoner with needlework, or musical instruments, or any other sedate entertainment with which she might wish to pass the time. But Kate, whose greatest pleasures were riding and walking, and who had no liking at all for sedentary amusements, found no possible consolation in her captor's thoughtfulness. She came to realise very quickly that the most trying aspect of her imprisonment was its tedium. Meals provided some diversion – they were ample and varied and well cooked – and when Marie Ange brought them Kate tried to keep her in conversation for as long as possible. But the maid had her work to do, and could spare little time for idle talk, and Kate would watch her go with regret, wishing she might be allowed to help with the cooking and cleaning, even if going out to the market would certainly be forbidden. When she plucked up courage at last to ask Marie Ange if she might come down to the kitchen, the maid looked deeply shocked.

'That is no work for a lady!' she exclaimed in horror. She doesn't know, Kate thought ruefully, how often I've been servant and mistress at one and the same time in my father's house, when he was on the run from his creditors and we had to fend for ourselves. But clearly that was something she could never make Marie Ange understand – certainly not in her own inadequate French – and she had to accept the irritating restrictions on her movements.

Sometimes, though, when there was a man about to keep watch on her, she was allowed to leave her room and descend to the rooms below, and even, after a time, to the green overgrown garden. It was too small and shut in to offer her the airy escape she longed for, but it was better than nothing. Its uncared-for state troubled her though. Somewhere beneath the luxuriant weeds roses grew, unpruned and half-choked, and a paved path had once run between neat beds. Faced with disorder, Kate's natural instinct had always been to set it to rights, as vigorously and as quickly as possible. But this was not her garden, and she was a prisoner, and it took her two days to pluck up courage to set to work. Marie Ange, laughing, supplied her with tools, and for a few days afterwards Kate was fully occupied and almost happy. At the end of the time the roses were blooming in weedless beds, a vine on a sunny wall had shot into new and healthy growth, and Kate found herself once more with nothing to do.

She wondered sometimes how long it would take for William to send her ransom. What if word came from him while the Captain was away? She had no idea where the *Marguerite* had gone, or how long she would be absent. Marie Ange steadfastly refused to discuss that matter at all. Kate wondered too, in her more pessimistic moments, what would happen if the Captain met his just deserts in some sea battle and did not return at all. Would they all forget she was here, and would she remain a prisoner for ever? But no, she told herself severely, William must soon know where she was, and he would not allow her to moulder in irksome captivity for ever.

Two weeks passed, with no news of the Captain or of Kate's ransom. Her French improved, aided by her unenthusiastic reading and her conversations with Marie Ange, who talked of her girlhood on a farm near the city, and her life since. Kate liked her stubborn common sense, her cheerfulness, her enjoyment of life. It was some consolation in the tedium of her imprisonment to feel that she had found a friend.

It was a hot Sunday morning and the bells of the city were clamorously calling the citizens to church when a commotion downstairs drew Kate to investigate. There were shouts, a cry of dismay from Marie Ange, doors slamming, running feet in the street outside. Kate descended cautiously, tracing the sound to the ground-floor room, and pushed open the door.

On a straw mattress placed hastily before the empty hearth lay the Captain, stretched full length, his head thrown back. There were too many people crowded round him for her to see more than a mass of tangled black curls spread upon the makeshift bed; and an ugly gaping wound in his thigh upon which a surgeon was working with concentrated urgency. At the foot of the bed, Marie Ange stood vigorously blowing her nose. That she had been crying was obvious, and also that she was trying to control herself so that she might be useful.

Kate stepped quickly into the room, and

stopped short as she came within sight of the Captain's face, grey and set, with closed eyes, like that of a man close to death.

'What happened?' she cried out. Unthinkingly she had spoken in English, so no one answered her. But they were in any case too concerned for the wounded man to pay her any attention. The room was crowded with anxious seamen, dirty and dishevelled and bloodstained, as if they had come straight here from whatever battle had proved their Captain's downfall. Kate wondered sickeningly, if the blood on their clothes was his.

With the utmost care the surgeon drew a musket ball from the wound, and then proceeded to bind it. Marie Ange was sent to bring blankets to cover her master; and the surgeon turned his head sufficiently to set eyes on a second woman, and said briskly: 'You – hold this!'

Kate came obediently and took the bowl he passed to her, and held it as he instructed beneath the Captain's arm while he was bled. She watched the operation with disfavour.

'He looks to me,' she thought, 'as if he'd lost more blood than he could spare already. I can't believe this will do him any good.' But it was not her place to argue with the experienced medical man, and she did as she was told; and when Marie Ange came with the blankets helped to cover the long motionless form, carefully, avoiding pressure on the wound. Looking down on him afterwards, it struck Kate with horrible force how still he was, how all that animal vigour had gone, all that energy and power, leaving only the still figure drained of colour and almost of life. Pity brought an obstruction to her throat, and tears to her eyes.

She stayed with Marie Ange when the surgeon had gone, watching for any signs of life. There had been an encounter at sea, the maid told her, and although the result had been a victory for the *Marguerite* the Captain had been hit. Sometimes the ship carried a surgeon, but not on this voyage, and there had been nothing for it but to return with all speed to St Malo. The surgeon this morning had shaken his head over the delay, but hoped that the Captain's youth and strength would be to his advantage. Now there was nothing for it but to wait and see.

It was a long anxious day. For most of it a small knot of sailors waited with the women, their painful anxiety contrasting curiously with their barbaric appearance. Everyone seemed to have forgotten that Kate was a prisoner, and thus supposed to regard the

Captain as an enemy. In fact, they seemed to have forgotten her presence completely.

By evening, when the surgeon called again, the Captain was showing signs of returning consciousness, though scarcely aware of where he was or who was with him. His men were sufficiently relieved to remember their responsibilities, and Kate was packed hastily off to her room with her supper and locked in.

She ate almost nothing and slept hardly at all afterwards. She lay open-eyed for much of the night, straining her ears for any sound which might tell her what was happening below. But apart from an occasional distant conversation, or the sound of someone moving quietly about, all was still. She had no news at all until late in the morning when one of the seamen came with her breakfast and told her that the Captain was a little feverish. When she asked if she might go down and offer her help to Marie Ange he ignored her, and the door was locked firmly once more.

That evening Marie Ange herself asked for help, and Kate hurried down to join her. The room was curtained now, and oppressively hot, for a great fire had been lit in the hearth. The sick man was motionless no more, and the grey colour had gone. In its place a hectic brightness flushed his cheeks and lit his dark eyes, and he stirred restlessly, muttering, shouting, pulling at the high-piled blankets that covered him. Marie Ange watched Kate as she noticed the change, and then, when the younger girl turned to meet her eyes, burst into tears.

Kate put an arm about her.

'You ought to go and rest,' she said gently. 'I don't believe you've slept at all since yesterday.' Marie Ange admitted the truth of that, and Kate offered, 'Let me stay and watch. I've nursed the sick before. My mother taught me well, and when she died I had to care for everyone at home. You can tell me what the surgeon said, and trust me to do the best I can.'

Marie Ange hesitated for a moment, torn between concern for her master and her own exhausted state; and then was on the point of leaving the Captain in Kate's care. But at that moment she remembered just in time that Kate was not simply a guest.

'No – I can't do that.' She shook her head vigorously. 'I can't leave you alone here.'

In case, thought Kate ruefully, I shall try and poison him, or do him some other harm. She protested that she wanted the

Captain well as much as anyone, for otherwise her return home might be indefinitely delayed. Marie Ange, whose instinct in any case was to trust her, gave in at last, on condition that one of the *Marguerite's* crew kept watch with her, and that she did not leave the room. If she wanted anything, the men would bring it, making sure she was never alone with the sick man. Having given the surgeon's instructions in detail, the servant took herself thankfully to bed.

Kate stood for a little while looking down at the Captain, raving in delirium. She laid a hand on his forehead, and was appalled at its heat. The roaring fire and the piled bedclothes must make it unbearable for him.

'I want cool water, lots of it, at once,' she instructed the man on guard, and after a moment's hesitation he called for it to be brought. But when she began to pull the blankets from the bed, leaving only a sheet covering the sick man, he protested sharply.

'I know what I'm doing,' Kate told him, stubborn and unmoved. 'I've nursed fevers before.' She did not pause to consider what would happen if, in spite of her treatment, the Captain grew worse. The surgeon had ordered that he be kept as warm as possible, and she was deliberately flouting his orders.

But for the moment she was thinking only of the patient.

When the water came she soaked a cloth in it and began to sponge the burning skin with it, the face and hands and body, and the long restless limbs. She let the fire die to a gentle glow, and when her cloth grew dry in the heat from the sick man's body, returned it to the water and began again. As she worked, her hands gentle and soothing, she talked in a soft voice as she might to a child, reassuring, comforting; and all the time she watched for any change, pausing now and then to feel the rapid uneven pulse.

At last, after about an hour, she thought she saw some little sign of improvement. The sick man grew quieter, calling out less wildly, and the heat of his skin was less intense. Very gradually his pulse slowed. And then the muttering ceased altogether, and his eyes rested on her face as if he knew her; and then he fell into a quiet sleep.

It was by no means over. Kate ceased her sponging for a little while; but late in the night the Captain grew restless again, and she began once more to cool the overheated skin. And then as dawn broke he fell at last into a deep untroubled sleep, and she began to hope that now the worst was past. When

Marie Ange came stumbling down the stairs, her face drawn with anxiety, her eyes went at once to the peaceful figure on the bed. For a moment she paused, caught between hope and fear. And then she saw how steadily and evenly he was breathing, and how the un-natural colour had gone from his face. Kate watched the relief spread over her features.

'God be praised!' exclaimed Marie Ange. The man on guard broke in to tell her the extent of Kate's responsibility for the improvement, and she laughed and hugged her, delighted that the surgeon had been proved wrong.

Fortunately perhaps, Kate had gone to her room to rest before the surgeon came again, so she did not hear what he said when he found that his instructions had been disobeyed. She slept deeply, secure in the certainty that the Captain would now recover. She was told that evening that he had woken once, and taken a little broth, and was now asleep again. Once, she heard Marie Ange singing, quietly, but with all her relief and thankfulness audible in her voice.

Next morning before breakfast Kate was astonished when the maid came, round eyed, and told her that the Captain wished to speak to her. With a heart beating suddenly almost as rapidly as if she too had a fever, Kate tidied her hair, and straightened her by now shamefully creased gown, and followed the maid down the stairs.

She was herself amazed at how quickly the Captain seemed to be recovering. A low folding bed had been set up now before the fire, and he lay supported on pillows, a little pale perhaps, but as alert and alive as she remembered him to have been at their first meeting. It was hard to believe that he had ever been so ill.

He dismissed Marie Ange and ordered Kate to take a seat on a chair near his bed, placed so that she would be facing him. He was smiling pleasantly, and Kate felt her colour rise as she sat down. She was no longer the calm and sensible woman in complete control of a difficult situation; no more than he was any longer the helpless invalid.

'I understand,' he began, once she had taken her seat, 'that I owe you thanks for your care of me. More – if Marie Ange is to be believed, I owe you also my life. For that I hope you will believe me most truly grateful.'

She was startled by the courteous formality of the tone, and even more by the words. He was not smiling now, was even frowning a little as if he was concerned to express himself as well as possible on so important a subject. Kate felt her colour deepen still further, and tried unsuccessfully to stammer out a reply.

'I do not remember well,' he broke in; and then, his voice, suddenly lower, and softening, 'but I heard, I think, a most gentle voice, and if it was the voice of my enemy, she had most kindly hands also.'

Kate looked down at the hands, twisted now in her lap, and was overcome with confusion. It was not simply his thanks, but the warmth of his tone, the astonishing depth of emotion in it, which moved her. She could think of nothing at all to say, or nothing that would not sound completely inadequate.

'I am glad,' she said eventually, in a voice which sounded horribly prim, 'that I was able to be of use.'

He laughed.

'How very English, Miss Pendleton!' And he held out his hand. Wonderingly, she laid hers in it, and his fingers closed about hers, strong and warm. A curious tingling impulse seemed to pass through her, running along her arm to her shoulder, finding its swift way to every part of her body. As so often before, she felt almost unable to breathe, as if his nearness shut out the air, and deprived her of any control over her muscles or her limbs. She felt an uncomfortable urge to laugh or to cry, she did not know which; and at the same time she could not quite do either. It was a relief, and also a loss, when after a moment he released her hand.

'I...' she began, not quite knowing what she meant to say; and realised he had also begun to speak at the same moment. She looked up, and they laughed, and he said: 'After you, mademoiselle'; and she said 'I can't remember what I meant to say,' and he confessed 'Neither can I,' and they laughed again. Then there came an odd uneasy silence, after which he asked abruptly. 'Your name – I do not know it. What do you call yourself?'

'Katherine – Kate,' she said quickly, a little surprised by the suddenness of the question.

'Ah!' he said with satisfaction, as if that somehow explained a great deal. 'Kate – Miss Kate Pendleton.'

The pronunciation delighted her, and she gave a gurgle of laughter, which she then found she had to explain. He frowned at her mock indignation.

'Then you shall say my name,' he decided. 'Come now: Tristan de Plouvinel. Let me hear you!'

She said it, but in her own neat English voice it sounded to her ears stiff and wooden. How much finer it had sounded in his deep musical tones! And it was a fine name, she reflected, like that of the hero of some old romance. Catching him watching her, as if reading her thoughts, she coloured again, and was annoyed with herself for being so easily embarrassed.

'So,' he said next, 'now we are friends. Do you not agree?'

She nodded, smiling.

'Yes,' she said, her voice emerging in a whisper.

At that charged moment Marie Ange came to announce the surgeon's arrival to dress the wound. The Captain scowled, and swore under his breath, but managed a brief parting smile for Kate.

'We shall talk again, shall we not, Miss Kate?' he said, as she smiled in return and left him to the surgeon's ministrations.

She found when she reached her room that her colour was still high, and her pulses racing. It was no fever that troubled her now, but something oddly like it, something that made her unable to think of anything at the moment but the man she had just left. He was so unlike any man she had met before – which was after all only to be expected, as her experience of pirates had been until recently non-existent. No, not pirates, she corrected herself with a little smile: corsairs. It had a grander ring, if the effect was much the same.

'How very silly,' she thought, crossing to the window and pushing it open. 'For that is all he is after all, call it what you will: a pirate. Why should I be in such a state about him? He is handsome, true – more handsome than any man I've known in my life – exciting and different, and dangerous. Perhaps that's it, that life has been so dull since Father died that I find danger attractive all at once. I shall have to pull myself together. This won't do at all.'

But by the time Marie Ange came, late in the afternoon, to summon her once more to the Captain's presence, she knew she scarcely had herself under control at all. And as she descended the stairs she found her heart was beating more quickly than ever.

'Do you play lansquenet?' he greeted her without preliminary as she came into the room. It had been her father's favourite game, and she nodded. 'Yes.'

'Then we shall play.' He instructed her to pull up a table, and bring the cards from a shelf at the far side of the room, and take her seat facing him. 'The surgeon commands rest, but I have slept too much already,' he told her. 'Now you will entertain me.'

She smiled pertly.

'You clearly want full value from me – a ransom *and* entertainment. All that, and a sick-nurse too. Are you not fortunate?'

Reminded of her recent care of him, he became suddenly grave, and his voice took on the warmth she remembered from this morning.

'More fortunate than I can say, mademoiselle,' he agreed.

It was a moment or two before his lighter mood returned and he began to distribute the cards. She watched the brown hands moving deftly and swiftly over the table, fascinated by their strength and agility. It was as if she could not fail to be wholly absorbed by the least thing he did; yet she had watched men dealing cards more times than she could remember, and never before found that single action worth watching with such close and total attention.

'Perhaps you will win back your ransom,' he suggested as they began to play; but she soon realised that he had no real fear of that. She played well, but there was never any likelihood that she would win. She was glad only that he did not beat her too quickly or too easily.

'You are a young woman of intelligence, I see,' he complimented her as he shuffled the cards at the end of the first game. 'I shall forgive you your debts.'

'Thank you,' she returned gravely, watching him. What kind of man was he really? she thought, and wondered again what had made him take up so dangerous and barbaric a career. In the end, gaining courage, she asked him outright.

He thought for a moment, a little surprised at the question, and then shrugged. 'Necessity, I suppose,' he said. 'It is a good way to make one's fortune, and I had none. Lands, yes, but too burdened by my father's debts to yield any fruits without the spending of much money. So, I became a corsair. It is, of course,' he added with a grin, 'a life which offers excitement, adventure, freedom also.'

'For you, but hardly for your victims,' she retorted disapprovingly.

'Oh? Is this not an adventure for you?'

That infuriating blush crept over her face.

'I am alive. But I am fortunate, I think. Not all your prisoners are used so kindly, are they, Captain?'

'Not all deserve it so well,' he returned gracefully.

'You mean not all can be exchanged for a rich ransom,' she told him, her tone sharp.

'You know that was not what I meant. Besides, it is a matter of fortune. All who go to sea take their chance. Sometimes they win, sometimes they lose, that is all. Let me tell you of this most recent fight, where I got this–' He gestured towards the wound. Then he gave her a lively account of the sea battle, in which it seemed the *Marguerite* had taken on two English men-of-war and emerged victorious. Kate noticed how the Captain's face reflected his words as he talked, vivid, alive, every passing emotion taking shape there before her eyes. He was a superb story-teller, his brown hands never still, his eyes bright, his brows lifting, then drawn together in a frown, and then that sudden heart-stopping smile lighting his dark face. But at the end of it Kate, unmoved for once, could think only of the *Proud Lady* and the scenes she had witnessed when the men from the *Marguerite* boarded her.

'It all sounds very heroic,' she commented drily. 'But you make no mention of preying on unarmed merchant ships. That is hardly heroic, and you can hardly call it a victory when the result is never in doubt.'

'We have to eat,' he said airily. 'A fat merchant ship will keep a man from want for many days.'

'And you never think of your victims, I suppose, and how it seems to them? I think it's mean, and cruel, and ignoble.' She watched as the defiant indignation of her tone reached him, and the black brows drew together in an angry frown.

'What do you know of poverty, and the necessity it forces upon a man?'

'A great deal,' she told him. 'But I would not stoop to that kind of solution, however great my need. I could not sleep easy in my bed afterwards.'

'You are a woman,' he said in a dismissive tone which infuriated her. Then before she could think of a suitable retort he went on: 'Come, let us have another game.'

She was tempted to refuse, so irritated was she; but something made her give in. After all, at least she was not bored, here with this man. As they played he talked lightly, coaxing her skilfully, almost without her knowing it, into a less critical frame of mind. They played three more games and then, to her astonishment, he lost the last. She looked at him with concern, noting the shadows about the dark eyes, and the renewed pallor.

'You're tired,' she said gently. 'You've done too much today. You must rest now, or I'll be in trouble with the surgeon.' She gathered up the cards, and returned the table to its place, and removed two of the pillows so that he could lie down. Then she straightened the blankets and tucked them about him. He watched her, smiling faintly.

'I see you feel your power over me,' he observed with wry amusement.

'But of course,' she agreed. 'Who would not revel in my position?' And then, moved by some inexplicable impulse, she bent and kissed him lightly on the forehead, as she would a child. She did not stay to see how he took it. In sudden horror at what she had done she turned quickly and ran from the room.

It was a long time that night before she ceased wondering what on earth had possessed her, and fell asleep with the question unanswered.

Five

When Marie Ange came next morning with Kate's breakfast, her expression was thoughtful.

'Monsieur le Capitaine asks to see you again when the surgeon has been,' she said. 'I am to come for you.' She paused, and stood looking at Kate, as if that might help her to understand what was going on. Finally she shook her head. 'I do not like it.'

'Why not?' asked Kate, more lightly than she felt. 'I have nothing to do, and nor has he, but everyone else is busy. Is it not logical that we should entertain one another?'

'Perhaps,' said Marie Ange, unconvinced. And as Kate made her way downstairs a little later she was not convinced either. Furthermore, she was hot with embarrassment at the thought of yesterday. What on earth would the Captain say to her today? And how could she possibly explain herself?

To her relief the Captain was in a vile temper and very far indeed from thinking of last night.

79

'That cursed surgeon commands me to lie in bed for yet one week!' he exclaimed. 'I am well, I tell him, but he does not listen! And then, he says that I must not go out even when I am not in bed – I must sit at home, and lean on a stick, and do nothing! *Mon Dieu,* how can I bear it!'

Kate laughed and pulled a chair to the bedside.

'It will be very good for you. Now you will know what it's like.'

His expressive hands ceased in mid-flight and fell to lie on the bedcovers.

'What *what* is like?' he demanded.

'To be shut in one place with nothing to do, no air, and no company but those in the house, and no freedom to do what you want. You are fortunate. I have already had three weeks of it.'

'You! But you are a woman – that is different.'

'Why is it different? I'm sure I hate being confined as much as you do.'

'That is not possible. A woman's world is in the home. She is by nature a creature confined – the kitchen, the hearth, the bedroom, the nursery – if she may not go to market for a little while, is that so very bad? Not, I think, as it is for a man for whom the whole earth is his territory.'

'My world,' said Kate emphatically, 'has never been the home. I hate being shut up. I like to ride and walk and be out and doing things. I have nearly gone mad locked up here with nothing to do but read and sew. I *hate* sewing!'

He gazed at her in such astonishment that she laughed.

'But how is that possible?' he demanded. 'Are you not a well-bred young lady?'

So she told him, in detail, of the years before her father died, the nomadic, impoverished, over-eventful childhood in which the deep love of her parents for each other and for their children had been the only stable element. Much of what she told was sordid, or unpleasant, or even painful, but she told it well and with humour, and the Captain laughed and prompted her to further tales. As a child she had learned by her father's example that laughter can add colour to what is drab and take the sting from misfortune. It was perhaps the best lesson her father could have taught her, and she wondered now if that was something the Captain knew too.

As she came to an end, he exclaimed through his laughter: '*Ah, ma belle,* but you are a great cure for boredom!' and she opened her eyes wide with astonishment.

Ma belle he had called her, and *belle* meant beautiful. No one had ever called her beautiful before, not even lightly and without thought as the Captain had done just now. And that had never surprised her, for she knew she was not beautiful. Now she put a hand to her face and wondered what the Captain had seen there that her mirror had never revealed to her. Or was he mocking her?

She had no means of knowing, for the next moment he said: 'Now, tell me – this gentleman in Ireland who is to be your husband – will he like to have a wife who wishes for adventure and does not care to sit at home and sew?'

Kate felt a great weight settle over her spirits, shutting out in a moment all the light-heartedness and wonder of a few minutes ago.

'He likes hunting,' she returned defensively; but she knew that her tone gave her away. She had not asked William's opinion, of course, but she knew quite well what kind of wife he wanted. And she knew that in doing her duty by him she would be turning her back on almost everything that had brought light and colour to her life in the days gone by. She could only hope that some quieter enjoyment would come in time to take its place.

The Captain looked at her intently for a moment or two, and then shrugged and said with a frown: 'So – there it is. Now let us play a game.' And she went obediently to bring up the table and cards. This time, to her amazement, she beat him on the second game, and knew she could not on this occasion attribute his failure to weariness. He was only too alert, glowering disbelievingly at her final winning hand.

'This I do not believe!' he exclaimed. 'You cheat, Miss Kate!'

'Indeed I do not!' she retorted indignantly. 'I have never cheated in my life. Don't judge others by yourself! *I* do not think any dishonesty is permitted so long as it brings me success.'

'And you say I do? You wrong me, Miss Kate, and that I will not have!'

'You're just a poor loser, that's all,' she told him severely. 'I didn't accuse you of cheating when you won.'

'That is because I am the better player.'

'Then let me enjoy my little triumph.' Her eyes sparkled with mischief. 'Now, is it not a good time to stop, while I am winning?'

He raised his hands expressively.

'*Mon Dieu,* you can ask that? No – let us begin again – I must have my revenge!'

When eventually Marie Ange interrupted them with dinner, he asked Kate to eat with him, and she agreed. She had forgotten what a delight it was to eat in agreeable company. 'It must be years,' she thought, 'since I have enjoyed a meal so much.'

That the Captain was almost well, and only his wound now kept him bedridden, was obvious to everyone. Daily he grew more restless, and more irritable. Often, shut in her room, Kate would hear him shouting at the servants, swearing, raging against the whole world. She felt quite sorry for the surgeon, for whom he reserved his most furious outpourings. Marie Ange ceased to look askance at Kate's daily descents to the Captain's bedside.

'At least it keeps his mind on something else for a while, and gives us some peace,' the maid observed with feeling.

Kate saw only too well what she meant when she came down one afternoon just before the week of lying in bed was over, to be met in the doorway by a book thrown with force at a fleeing servant: it only just missed her, and it was heavy. A torrent of thunderous French followed it. The Captain's eyes were ablaze with fury, his anger filling the room. Kate stood in the doorway and began to laugh.

The swearing stopped, abruptly. The Captain stared at her, and then he said: 'How dare you laugh! I cannot tolerate this … this…' His English failed, and he started again. 'You see they do not wait to answer me! They run away–'

'I'm not surprised,' said Kate. 'If you're throwing any more books I shall go too.'

'No – do not do that. Stay and fight with me!'

She closed the door and came to the bedside.

'Patience is not your strong point, is it?' she asked. He frowned.

'Do not lecture me, English Miss Kate. When you do so you look so very much like a well-bred young lady.'

She laughed.

'Then I'll beat you at cards and show you how very badly brought up I am.'

She turned away to bring the table, but he caught her arm in a grasp which had no weakness in it at all; and then he pulled her near until she found herself sitting on the edge of the bed. And before she knew what was happening he had clasped her in his arms, and brought his mouth down on hers and was kissing her as no one in all her life had ever kissed her before. She did not even dream of resisting him. Just for a moment surprise stilled her and then with a strange sense of inevitability – even of rightness – she put her arms about him and gave herself up to his embrace. For that long moment there was nothing and no one that mattered but this, that she was in his arms and all the strength and power of his great body was concentrated in his kiss; and that she yielded to him with all her heart. She felt one of his hands run down her back to her waist, the other slide into her hair. She felt a sweet melting delight run through her limbs, drawing her ever nearer to him. She knew she wished that it would never end.

And then as suddenly as it had begun it did end. He almost thrust her from him, as if that was the only way he could release her. And then he held her at bay, staring at her, breathing fast, his eyes darker than ever beneath his frowning brows.

'I give you my most humble apologies, Miss Kate,' he said stiffly after a moment, his voice still rough with emotion. His hands fell from her arms, and she stood up, smoothing her gown; not because she wanted to place a safe distance between herself and him, but because she knew it was expected of her. 'I did not intend that to happen,' he went on. 'You see, it is a long time since I had – the company – of a woman–'

She knew full well that 'company' was not what he meant. She had a sudden vision of what exactly he did mean, and for an instant saw herself as the woman, and could not bear to look at him for the aching longing which filled her. She had never known this feeling before. She knew how children came, she knew what a wife's duties were, she knew something of what had passed between her brother and his women friends, in years gone by; but this desperate passion was new to her, new and for the moment almost beyond bearing. She pressed her hands tightly together and turned away from the bed and walked to the window. Tristan de Plouvinel read offended virtue in every step.

'Miss Kate – I would not lose a friend. Say you understand – and put it from your mind.'

Her mouth twisted in a rueful ghost of a smile. She could never put that from her mind, even less from her body, tingling still from his touch. But moved by the faintly pleading note in his voice she drew a deep breath and tried as best she could to bring herself under control, and carried the card table briskly to its usual position, firmly between them.

'It's all forgotten,' she lied. 'Say no more. I understand.' That last at least was true; she did understand. Her mother had taught her about men's needs, as had her observations of her brother Harry. Captain de Plouvinel was like any other man, with nothing much to do and no woman at present in his bed. It had happened that Kate Pendleton was there, and so Kate Pendleton had been the one to tempt him to that moment of weakness. And now Kate Pendleton would have to be very sensible and pretend that it had never happened.

This time when they played cards he won easily, and began to lose his temper with her because she was so preoccupied and so lacking in her usual ready talk and laughter. She was not in a very good humour herself by the time she left him.

She hardly slept at all that night, and was glad that the next day was to be the Captain's first day out of bed. He spent the

88

morning with a manservant for company taking his first steps across the room, and by the time he sent for her in the afternoon was tired by his exertions, chastened by finding how inadequate his legs felt when he tried to use them again. The servants had enjoyed a quiet day.

He was sitting in an armchair near one of the windows looking over the garden when she came in, a brocaded silk dressing-gown thrown loosely over his ruffled shirt and plum-coloured breeches. He held a book in his lap, but did not appear to have been reading it. In fact she thought his eyes were closed as she came in, though he opened them almost at once, and smiled.

'You see, I am recovered now,' he said. 'I mark my recovery by renouncing cards for today. Come and sit down and we shall talk.'

She wondered if he had forgotten yesterday's incident completely. If he had not, then it clearly meant nothing to him at all, for no awareness of it marked his expression or his voice. She felt a little hurt that it should be so, but had to admit that it made it easier for them both.

'What are you reading?' she asked as she sat down on the window seat nearby.

'Poetry,' he said briefly, laying the book

aside. 'But I am not in the mood. I do not read very much. I like poetry best in dramatic form, presented as a play. Such as the work of Monsieur Molière, performed so often at court– That is amusing, too.'

'You go to court sometimes!' she exclaimed.

'But of course. I am a faithful servant of my king. Did I not tell you that?– Do you care for the theatre, Miss Kate?'

'It's a very long time since I've seen a play – not since my father was alive. I don't remember anything very well – though there was an old fashioned play by a Mr William Shakespeare, now long dead, which I liked once very much–'

'Ah, did he not write of a Kate? I remember – there was a play which concerned a wild woman of that name, who must be tamed. Does that not strike a chord?'

She gave him a mock-angry look.

'Should it? I can't think why– Now, is there a Tristan somewhere in some play? I remember the name, I think, but I'm not sure–'

'You are thinking perhaps of the old tale – a sad and beautiful one, mademoiselle. It tells how Tristan was sent to Brittany to bring to King Mark his bride Iseult and how

90

on the voyage over the sea Tristan learned himself to love Iseult, and she him – and so they were doomed, for their love was forbidden. You hear in my name, Miss Kate, the echoes of a tragic passion.'

Something unreadable in his expression held her gaze. She sat quite still looking into the dark eyes, holding her breath. It was as if he wished to tell her something of enormous importance.

But it must have been an illusion, for the next moment he looked away, and shifted a little uncomfortably in his chair, and then laughed.

'But what are stories, Miss Kate, when there is life to be lived? I shall be thankful indeed when I can leave this room and return to sea.'

For some reason Kate did not want to think of that.

'Have you heard from William – from Mr Harwood – yet?' she asked. 'About the ransom, I mean.'

She had a distinct if momentary impression that he had completely forgotten until then that she was his prisoner. But he collected his thoughts, and said: 'No – no, not yet, Miss Kate. It always takes time.'

So she was, presumably, not his first prize.

She wondered who the others had been, but thought perhaps it was better not to know. Instead, she encouraged her companion to tell her more of his adventures, and soon found herself wrapped in the excitement of what he had to say.

That evening in her room she stood for a long time at the window watching the sun sink fierily into the sea. And she found after a time that she was whispering to herself, murmuring over and over the lilting musical name of her captor, as she might recite a line of poetry or a charm.

'Tristan de Plouvinel. Tristan de Plouvinel.'

Six

The Captain quickly regained his strength. The folding bed was put away, once he could negotiate the stairs to his own room on the first floor. Kate was less in demand, since he was more easily able to amuse himself. And his temper improved as the prospect of returning to sea became more real.

Though Kate saw less of him, she was invited to come down each evening to share supper with him, and often they would sit talking for hours afterwards, long after the dishes had been cleared and the wine drunk and dusk had fallen. In his company she did not hear the curfew warning the citizens to go home to their beds, or the distant barking of the dogs released on to the rocks. She was forgetful of everything but the swiftly changing moods reflected on his expressive face and in the graceful movements of his eloquent hands; and the delight of his conversation, lively, unpredictable, dramatic, or hilariously funny, every story told in the deep voice she would have been happy to listen to for ever and ever. When at last one or other of them became suddenly aware that it was too dark to make out the corners of the room, or that the ornate clock stood at close on midnight, then Kate would never fail to be astonished that time could pass so quickly, and she would leave the room with an enormous reluctance.

Now and then, he summoned her to cards, and that was better still, for she would stay till supper time and after, and there would be even longer in which to enjoy his company. She had forgotten that she had ever been bored.

Then, one day as they sat at cards, a liveried messenger came riding to the house, weary and travel-stained and bearing a letter. Kate was banished at once to her room, and heard no more until the Captain summoned her early next morning.

She came into the room expecting to see him, as usual, lounging at ease in his dressing gown, or in shirt and breeches, for the day was already hot. Instead his appearance brought her to an immediate halt.

He stood by the fire, so magnificent a figure that for a moment, almost, she scarcely knew him. Gone was all trace of the pirate captain

94

and, too, of the relaxed companion of the past weeks. In its place stood an apparition resplendent in full court dress, the lace ruffles, the silk shirt, the coat of richly embroidered crimson and the full matching breeches, silken stockings and high-heeled beribboned shoes. In one hand he held fringed gloves and a feathered tricorn hat. At least, Kate thought bleakly, viewing this elegant stranger, he was not wearing the full-flowing wig which most fashionable gentlemen of her acquaintance would have worn. Perhaps in his trade a wig would be an inconvenience, and in any case his own thickly curling hair was as full and flowing as any wig.

He came towards her, and smiled, and was at once much more like the delighted companion she had come to know.

'I wished you to come, Miss Kate,' he said, 'because I find I must go to court. The King summons me to Versailles. And I wished to say some things to you before I left.'

Kate stared at him in dismay. The king's new palace of Versailles was a long way from St Malo. Inevitably he would be gone for several days, at the very least.

'First, I wish to thank you for helping to pass the time so agreeably of late. I am grateful – I do not find it easy to be tied by the heels–'

For a moment she had forgotten his recent wound. Now she broke in anxiously: 'But are you fit to travel? You have not been out yet – I'm sure the surgeon would say–'

'The devil take the surgeon!' he exclaimed with a laugh. 'I do not need him any more. Nor,' he went on, smiling down at her, 'do I need your nursing now, grateful though I was for it. But if it reassures you, I go to the mainland by boat, and from there I travel in my own coach, in comfort. See what very good sense I have!'

Kate found that she could not manage a smile. She felt as if a leaden lump had settled inside her, weighing on her spirits, bringing her firmly back to the drab reality from which the last few weeks had lifted her.

'I have given instructions,' the Captain went on, 'that you are to be treated with great courtesy. You are free to move about the house as you wish. You may also go into town, so long as you are escorted. You have sense enough I think not to attempt an escape. The watchmen will know if you go by day – and at night–' He gave a wave of one beringed hand. Then his eyes ran over her, and Kate was all at once aware of the appalling state of her clothes. 'You may wish perhaps to make for yourself a gown – Marie Ange sews well, so she may help. I know you do not care to sew.' He smiled faintly, teasing her, but she had no answering smile for him. 'Marie Ange will help also if you need money – as will Hervé, who is to remain in charge here.' Hervé, Kate knew, was the scar-faced sailor who had brought her here that first day. 'As for your William – if word comes from him, it can await my return. I shall not be away, I think, for more than two weeks.'

Kate reflected that William would not have liked to hear his name on Captain de Plouvinel's lips. Pronounced by him it sounded somehow faintly ridiculous. And then she thought: 'Two weeks! It is a lifetime.'

The Captain must have been expecting her to say something, for he was silent for quite a long time, watching her. Eventually he said: 'I did not compliment you on your achievements in my little garden. You are free to do what you will there. Marie Ange will bring you flowers to plant if you wish.'

'Thank you,' said Kate stiffly, and there was another little silence, while they looked at each other. 'I wish you would hold me,' Kate was thinking. 'I cannot bear to part

97

like this. I wish you would kiss me again, like you did that day–' And then, recollecting herself, she blushed furiously and bent her head.

'Well, let it be *"au revoir"* then,' said the Captain at last. He gave a small bow, and Kate realised she was being dismissed.

'Goodbye,' she croaked, in an almost inaudible voice, and left the room.

Upstairs, she sat on her bed and gave way to slow and miserable tears. Through it all a little voice somewhere within her cried to the departing Captain: 'I love you! I love you!'

During the following days she had too much time to think, and for the most part her thoughts were not cheering. It might be expected, of course, that she would not be happy, as a helpless prisoner waiting to be ransomed. But that aspect of her plight was no longer of any importance to her at all. She knew now that she was in a very real sense a prisoner of quite another kind, and from this captivity there was no hope of ransom. Tristan de Plouvinel held her heart captive more surely than he held her person, and it was unlikely that he even guessed at his power over her. She remembered ruefully the talk of the silly female cousins with whom she had spent some time since her father's death. Full of foolish romanticism, they had imagined themselves in just such a situation as she was in now – captured by a highwayman, perhaps, or some other outlawed vagabond. Their captor was always handsome and ruthless and wildly attractive, and an inevitable passionate love ensued. Kate had despised such talk. And yet only a short time later here she was in love with a pirate Captain who had taken her prisoner!

But she knew it was nothing like her cousins' schoolgirl fantasies, for this was real. True, her Captain was handsome and strong and immediately attractive. But it was not for that she loved him, though that must play a part in it. What she loved was the man she had come to know over the past weeks, the lively companion, the quick-tempered emotional laughing human being beneath the splendidly romantic exterior. And it was that man she missed so desperately now.

'You're a fool!' she told herself. 'All he sees is a pleasant way of passing the time – someone to share a game of cards or a talk.' But he had called her 'ma belle', and kissed her, and told her of Tristan's tragic passion – was it possible–? She dared not answer 'yes', but sometimes when she thought of the hours they had shared so delightedly a little flame of hope rose and glowed within her. It was *just* possible – if only he would come back soon!

Seized by a hunger for any crumb which might bring him to mind, she encouraged Marie Ange and Hervé to talk of their Captain. Marie Ange was by far the better company of the two, and Kate did not greatly care for Hervé, who seemed much more like her idea of a pirate than did Tristan de Plouvinel, but the seaman had inevitably a far greater knowledge of his Captain than did the maid. Kate spent as much time with him as she could, always steering the conversation in the same direction.

Hervé was in some ways an unsatisfactory conversationalist. His information about the Captain was spare and factual. There were no dramatic tales of courage, no heartfelt expressions of admiration or affection. But Kate did learn a great deal, some of which surprised her, and some of which she wished afterwards she had not heard. It was Hervé, for instance, who told her that the Captain was in fact of an old noble Breton family, and by rights Comte de Plouvinel. Somewhere in the west a tumbledown manor marked the spot where he was born; that, and the lands around it, were still in his possession. It was their poverty which had driven him to sea.

'It must cost a great deal to equip a ship like the *Marguerite*,' commented Kate reflectively. 'Is it the King's ship?'

'Ah, no, mademoiselle. The *Marguerite* is named for the lady who equipped her and provided the cash for her to go to sea, and for her Captain too: Marguerite, Marquise de Tacoignières, a great lady to whom our Captain owes all his wealth and prosperity.'

'Oh,' said Kate, swallowing hard and staring out of the window. 'Is she – is she still alive?'

'But of course. Very likely our Captain is even now in her company. Their – collaboration – is an old one, and a close one, shall we say.'

Kate swallowed again.

'Is … is she beautiful? and young?'

'She is ageless, mademoiselle,' said Hervé, watching her intently. 'A little older perhaps than Monsieur le Comte, but she has a beauty that age cannot destroy. And, too, great charm and greater influence at court.'

'So that,' thought Kate dismally, 'is that. I was just an agreeable pastime for him. And it's over – only there never was anything to be over. He is now with the beautiful Marguerite for whom he named his ship, and it is unlikely that he has even given me a second thought. His only concern now will be to get me ransomed as soon as possible.'

It was a concern that, deprived in one blow of any hope that Tristan de Plouvinel might return her love, Kate came to share. The day's activities – even with her greater freedom – lost any interest for her. Everything became all at once grey and drab and tasteless. Often, for no apparent reason at all, she dissolved into tears. She felt weary and miserable and wanted only to leave this place, wishing most of all that her path had never crossed with that of Tristan de Plouvinel. Her heart ached ceaselessly and unbearably.

She stood one day in the downstairs room leaning on the window seat with her head pressed to the window, and stared unseeing out at the garden, grey and sodden in the drenching rain. She heard someone come in, and guessed it was Hervé, but did not bother to look round. She was not in the mood for company.

'You are not happy, I think, mademoiselle,' the sailor observed gently, coming towards her.

'What do you expect, shut up here a

prisoner away from my family and friends and–?' No, she thought, breaking off, not from 'everyone I love'. She felt the tears spring to her eyes.

'Of course,' said Hervé soothingly. 'That I understand. Perhaps I can help.'

She looked at him curiously, but said nothing, and after a moment he went on, lowering his voice to an undertone. 'Have you thought of escape?'

Her eyes widened. 'With those dogs out there, and the guards? I'd be stupid to try. I shall just have to wait for the ransom to come.'

'That could take a long time,' Hervé observed. 'I know – I have seen it happen before. There are so many arrangements to be made – the amount, the place for the exchange – and then the weather can be difficult. Sometimes it is a matter of years before a prisoner is released. If you could escape you might be home much more quickly. Once away from the city it would be easy to find a boat, especially with money, or a friend–'

'And I have neither,' said Kate. But she was staring at him, realising suddenly that he was not simply speculating, but deliberately offering her an opportunity.

She was silent for a moment, then she asked slowly: 'But why? Why do you want to help me?'

The sailor's mouth hardened.

'I have seen too much of our Captain's ways – his carelessness of human life, and human feelings. And we his men receive little enough of the rewards such behaviour brings him. It would please me to see him lose a ransom, when he was so sure of it.'

The malice in Hervé's tone was distasteful, but Kate did not pause to consider that. She knew suddenly that to escape from here was what she wanted more than anything else in the world. If she could have been sure that William's ransom would come very soon, then she would have waited. But if Hervé was right, that was very unlikely. And she had no wish at all to linger here for months or even years, faced with the unbearable pain of the Captain's nearness, knowing that she had no hope of being more to him than an amusing means of passing the time. The sooner she left all this behind her and learned to forget, the better.

So she turned to Hervé now, and said quietly, 'Tell me what I must do.'

Seven

If Tristan de Plouvinel had been blind and deaf he would still have known where he was the instant he reached Versailles. Its unmistakable smell would have told him that: the pungent unpleasant mingling of perfume and unwashed bodies and excrement – for the sanitary arrangements were both primitive and inconveniently placed. Now, in the intense heat of mid-August it was worse than ever. The King liked fresh air, favouring open windows even on the coldest winter days, but nothing could have rid his palace of its distinctive stench.

Finding release from it, when he could, in the vast and elaborate formal gardens, Tristan remembered how much he disliked Versailles. Once, with other courtiers, he had wondered why the King had not chosen the château of St Germain as his country residence, since he wished to establish his court well away from the murderous Paris rabble which had so disrupted his boyhood. St Germain, set in its great forest, looking out over the winding course of the river Seine, had been the favourite spot of successive Kings of France, and had every advantage, in its views and its situation and its healthy air. Instead, King Louis had chosen Versailles, site only of a primitive hunting lodge of his father's, barren of everything but bog and scrub, without forest or water, and notoriously unhealthy. Wiser now, Tristan, like many others, understood the king's choice. To take a fine château in a fine position and improve it offered no challenge at all to its owner. But to create the most splendid of palaces in a barren wilderness was an action worthy of the greatest monarch France had ever known, reflecting nothing but glory on that man. It was a monument to his splendour alone.

So here it was, almost complete, the elaborate court of which King Louis was the glorious centre, drawing to him all the men and women of wealth and power and influence in the land, protected alike from the seething rabble of the Paris streets, and the impoverished peasants of the countryside. Tristan wondered sometimes if the king knew anything at all of the lives of his ordinary subjects, men like the seamen who sailed with the *Marguerite*, or women like sturdy sensible Marie Ange. It was as if they lived in a different world from that of their king. Tristan thought longingly of the clear exhilarating air of St Malo; even the softer air of the place where he was born, tranquil amongst its fields and woodlands – though it was a very long time since he had been there.

It was some time before he was able to discover why the King had summoned him to court. The elaborate daily rituals of Versailles closed about him, their crowded formality making it impossible to have a quiet word with the monarch at their centre. He tried to gauge whether the summons indicated approval, or the reverse. At the King's *coucher* on his first evening at Versailles, he was permitted to hold the royal candlestick. That, he knew, was a rare and much sought-after honour, given only to the most highly favoured. He stood holding the elaborate candlestick aloft as the king undressed – assisted by this courtier and that – and prepared himself for bed; and wondered whether there was some other motive for the king's choice. Sometimes, he believed, a courtier with whom the king had a personal quarrel was favoured in some way simply so that others at court should not know of the quarrel. Could this be the case now? Certainly, with his leg aching after a day over-strenuous for one newly risen from a sick bed, there was no great pleasure in standing patiently by throughout the long ceremonious bedding of his king. Marguerite de Tacoignières might have been able to tell him why he had been summoned, but calling at her rooms this morning he had been told she was indisposed and could not see him for a day or two. That too might or might not be a worrying sign. Things were rarely simple or straightforward at court. There were too many couriers intriguing for the king's favour for that to be so.

The following evening the king sent for him to the apartment of Madame de Maintenon, where he most often conducted business these days. There the king's most long-serving mistress – now, in secret, his wife – sat quietly at one side of the fireplace, plain, respectably dressed, her attention apparently given to her sewing. Opposite her sat the king. Tristan bowed and stood waiting for the king to speak, watching intently for the frown or the smile which might help him understand why he was here. The King looked up at last from the table set before him, and he was smiling.

'Please be seated, my friend,' he said pleasantly. To be asked to sit in the king's presence was so great an honour that Tristan felt encouraged. He perched rather uncomfortably on the low stool placed near the king's chair, and waited again. For a moment he was aware of Madame de Maintenon's eyes raised from her sewing to look at him; but that was the only acknowledgement she gave of his presence throughout the interview, though he knew that her opinion of him could be of the utmost importance.

'We trust you are fully recovered from your wound, Monsieur le Comte,' said the king next, all affability. Tristan bowed his head to acknowledge the courteous enquiry.

'Yes, I thank you, sire.'

'It was won in a noble cause,' the king went on. 'We are fully sensible of your great services to France.'

So he had been summoned to be praised, even thanked! It was a long way to come for such a slight purpose, particularly when he was so newly recovered from his wound, but the king liked to remind his courtiers that they depended on his good opinion of them for their future prosperity.

The carefully chosen words of praise and

royal gratitude continued for a few moments, and then the king said suddenly: 'There is, however, another matter which has come to our attention.'

At once Tristan became alert. So there *was* something of which the king did not approve! He searched around for a clue as to what it might be, but his conscience was as clear as it was ever likely to be. True, there were prizes which he had taken from time to time and which had not found their way into the official records; but then the king was reasonable enough to recognise that a man must have his rewards if he was to give his services cheerfully.

'You have a young English lady as a hostage, have you not?'

To his annoyance, Tristan found himself colouring. 'Yes, sire, that is so,' he said cautiously. Clearly the king had decided this time that he was not going to be reasonable.

'That,' the king assured him, 'would not as a general rule trouble us. However, it seems that this particular young lady has a kinsman at the court of our dear cousin, the King of England.'

'Our cousin the King of England' was not, Tristan knew, the man William who at present occupied the throne and the royal palace in London, but the exiled King James lodged at St Germain. King Louis would never bring himself to speak so affectionately of King William, for whom he had a personal dislike to add to his distaste for him as a usurper.

Tristan also guessed, very quickly, who the kinsman at St Germain must be. Kate had told him a great deal about her beloved brother.

'Our cousin the King of England,' King Louis went on, 'did us the honour of dining with us last week; and it seems he has come to hear of the plight of this–' His eyes travelled to a paper on the table before him '–Miss Pendleton. On behalf of her brother, he begs most earnestly for her instant release. Such, as you know, is our affection for our cousin that we, your king, command it too. The young lady must be brought with all speed to her brother's care. Is that understood?'

There was a steely note beneath the king's courteous phrases. Tristan cursed whatever informant had told the king of Kate's presence at St Malo – the king's spies were notoriously efficient – but could only smile and agree that Kate should be released at the earliest opportunity. Once his agreement was given, the king was once more all affability, the matter passed over as a slight if regrettable error of judgement.

Marguerite had recovered from her indisposition – a summer cold – and he was admitted to her presence next morning. Powdered, perfumed, rouged, magnificently dressed, she received him in her gilded bedchamber, and accepted his kiss of greeting with her usual cool satisfaction.

'You have seen His Majesty, I suppose?' she asked, once the polite exchanges were over, and refreshments had been brought. 'Did he speak of the girl?'

'Then you know about her!'

'Of course. I have to keep myself informed as to the progress of my investments.'

Tristan paused, a sweetmeat half way to his mouth, and stared at her.

'What do you mean?' he asked slowly. 'How do you "keep yourself informed"?'

He thought that somewhere beneath the powder and rouge she had coloured slightly, but he could not be sure.

'Oh, I have friends at St Malo. You must know that surely? In any case, my friends are yours, are they not?'

Sudden rage left Tristan speechless. So she spied on him – and not only did so, but openly admitted it! And he had not once, in all the years he had known her, suspected it. She at least knew him well enough to interpret the sparkle in his dark eyes correctly.

'You are angry,' she said soothingly, 'but you should not be. You know I have your interests at heart. If I watch over you like the old friend I am, then what have you to complain of? Now I have I think preserved you from committing a folly which might have damaged your reputation with the king. The girl's name struck a chord, the moment I heard it. I remembered that when once a party came from St Germain I had made the acquaintance of a young gentleman in the English King's entourage, one Henry Pendleton. So I made enquiries – and the rest you know.'

'You mean you made sure they all knew where Miss Pendleton was, so that King James would be certain to ask for her return! – but why, in heaven's name? Why should you wish to deprive me of a ransom? Without your interference no one would have been any the wiser – and I have always given you a just share of any returns, have I not?'

'It is as well, I think, that you should be reminded now and then to whom you owe your present position,' said Marguerite with acid sweetness. 'Besides, you were becoming over familiar with the girl and I feared a delay in payment–'

'Dear God, can I keep nothing secret from you! What else do you know of my life – what I eat for breakfast each day? How many times I glance at the clock?'

She gave a tight little smile.

'Did I not say, I like to be informed?'

'You do not own me!'

'Do I not? How else would you have gone to sea, if it had not been for me?'

'And I have repaid you a hundredfold for that. I owe you gratitude, certainly – but I think I have even paid that debt by now.'

He looked at her, seeing her all at once with new eyes. And he knew that the gratitude which had kept him loyal to her all these years had been utterly misplaced. If she had helped him with money and influence in his early years it had been for her own ends only, and never for him. He had been flattered at fifteen, fresh from the country, innocent, poor, and very ignorant of the ways of the court, when this mature and beautiful widow had set out to seduce him, introduced him to the arts of love in which she was so very experienced, and then, later, when his father died, equipped a ship so that he might seek his fortune at sea, as he so much longed to do. But it had taken him until now, ten years afterwards, to realise that he had been simply her plaything, one amusement among many to alleviate the boredom of her days. Now, looking at her, he wondered that he could ever have thought her beautiful. She had not been young when he first knew her, but now she was old indeed, raddled and made ugly by the years of self-indulgence and intrigue, an ugliness which no amount of paint could hide. For the first time in years he thought of his mother as he had seen her last, just before her death, her hair white, her body bent, her skin lined, yet more radiantly beautiful in her old age than this woman had ever been. And then he thought of Kate, with her blushes and her freckles and her untidy hair, and a great wave of disgust swept him.

'You sicken me!' he exclaimed. 'You think of no one but yourself – you are like everyone here – greedy, selfish, heartless, and blind – blind to everything beyond these gilded stinking walls!'

Her colour had risen now, and her pale eyes were sparkling with indignation.

'And are you so selfless to speak to me like that? Have you not been feathering your own nest all these years, at the expense of anyone who crosses your path? Beware, my friend – if the King makes peace with England, as they say he must, you may find you need me again – but after this I shall not be so easily won over!'

Already half way to the door, Tristan paused and swung round.

'What did you say? Is there indeed talk of peace?'

Marguerite shrugged.

'The King must make peace, if war is not to ruin him. If it had not been for his loyalty to King James, and his great dislike of King William, a treaty would have been drawn up long ago. France needs peace, if you do not. You will have to accept that – and then what will you do, when there are no enemy ships for you to prey upon? How will you live, if you do not have me to speak for you?'

'Out in the open air, in freedom!' he retorted, and left the room, banging the door behind him. He knew she would never forgive him for that discourtesy.

He left Versailles next day, having taken his leave of the King and promising again to send Kate to St Germain. Yesterday's anger was still with him, setting his thoughts whirling in furious turmoil through his head. It was not simply that he was losing a ransom because of the machinations of Marguerite, though that was bad enough; or even that the pleasant interlude with Kate must come to an end. Once at St Germain she would certainly be returned to her sorrowing fiancé, and that would be that; whereas she might have spent months still at St Malo waiting for her ransom. But he could bear that. What angered him most of all was Marguerite's interference, and her admission that she had her spies at St Malo.

Was it one spy, or many? he wondered now. And who among those who served him was in her pay? He had thought them all totally loyal, wholly devoted to him. And now to know that one at least among them had been reporting on his every move so that it could be used against him–! It was intolerable. It must at least be someone who had lived under the same roof with him during the weeks of his illness, for the informant had reported on his 'familiarity' with Kate. It made his blood boil that even his hours of relaxation should be watched from Versailles by those greedy possessive eyes. Who was her spy? Marie Ange, the sturdy peasant woman who kept house for him, and whom he had regarded for so long as a friend? He hoped not, fervently he hoped not, yet it must be someone, and someone he liked and trusted. He swore that when he reached St Malo, before ever he carried out the King's orders and sent Kate to St Germain, he would find out. And there would be no mercy for Marguerite's spy.

As he came at evening within sight of St Malo his anger evaporated. Across the wide stretch of water, dark against the evening sun, the city rose, edged with silver where the waves broke foaming against the rocks and the ramparts at its feet. He could hear the noise of their crashing even as far away as this. He stepped from his coach into the waiting boat, and the sharp clear wind blew in his face, and tugged at his embroidered coat, and drove out any thought but his gladness in being back here, among his own kind. He thought, with a sudden impatience to be home, of Kate coming into the room to greet him, smiling that mischievous gap-toothed smile. He would not, he decided, send her to St Germain under escort as he had intended, but accompany her there himself, enjoying for as long as possible her lively and stimulating company. She was an unusual young woman. He would miss her when she had gone.

Marie Ange met him at the door, and her face was white.

'Oh, Monsieur le Capitaine, we tried to send word to you. She had gone, monsieur, two days ago – and Hervé with her!'

Eight

There was little anyone could tell Tristan. Kate and Hervé had disappeared one evening after dark when the household was asleep – or at least, Kate's room had been found empty next morning, and Hervé's bed had not been slept in. Later, a rope ladder had been found hanging forlornly from the ramparts, the sole witness to a flight whose sequel was unknown.

Tristan felt himself go cold with horror. He knew why they had chosen that night in particular for their flight, because it was one of the few occasions in the year when the tide came high enough to flood the rocks and keep the dogs at bay. But many times Tristan himself had seen that same tide at work, sending great crashing waves towering over the walls with a force that neither man nor beast could withstand. What could have driven Hervé, experienced seaman that he was, to take that desperate course? Kate's urgent persuasion? But he, Tristan, would not have allowed her at any price to urge him to a course so dangerous, and so surely doomed. Only a man who was desperate himself would have considered it for a moment.

Was Hervé desperate? Did he have cause to fear Tristan's return? Could he be Marguerite's spy, knowing by some sure instinct that he was on the verge of discovery, and justly fearing Tristan's anger? It was possible. It was some kind of explanation.

But it brought no comfort. Tristan stood shivering in the living room of his house and thought how empty it seemed, and wondered what he had done to make Kate so miserable that she should wish to put herself in Hervé's hands. She did not seem unhappy.

And where did that frail rope ladder lead? To what dark end? He knew what the sea could do, only too well. What had those powerful waves carried from the city walls that night? Did Kate's slender supple body lie even now stiff and cold and battered on some far shore? Marie Ange said they had found nothing, but they had not searched very far.

With a new grim light in his eyes Tristan turned suddenly, and called for his cloak and set out at once for the mainland. Somehow he must find out what had become of the bright-eyed laughing girl he might never see again.

The escape had begun encouragingly enough. Kate and Hervé had managed to creep from the house without being observed or followed, and made their way softly, keeping to the shadows, on to the ramparts. There was no moon, and so in the streets it was very dark indeed.

It was not until they reached the walls that Kate managed to place the distant roar which had caught her ears on their way from the house. And then as they took the last step on to the wide pathway a great drenching fount of spray crashed over the parapet and soaked her in an instant to the skin. It was at that moment that Kate first began to guess what she had let herself in for.

There on the walls with the waves roaring in her ears and crashing in towers of spray against the ramparts, her first and urgent impulse was to say to Hervé that she had changed her mind and wished to go back. Only a fool would risk trying to cross that wild tumultuous sea, a fool or a desperate man. An aching heart was not reason enough to drive her to this.

Then she reminded herself that Hervé was not a desperate man either, and he knew the sea. It was weak of her to lose her nerve when he had assured her that she was safe in his hands. She must trust him. So she drew a deep and steadying breath and followed him meekly along the walls, telling herself that at least they would be safe from the dogs tonight. At one point she thought she heard, faint and distant, the sound of barking, but for the most part the noise of the sea was too great for anything else to be audible. And it was quite clear that until the tide turned there was no chance that the dogs would be running free.

They came at last to a bastion jutting out into the sea, and here Hervé led her to its outermost edge and peered over.

'There!' he called above the roar. Kate looked, and could just make out, bobbing wildly on the water, the small black outline of a boat. It looked no more substantial than a leaf tossed on that raging sea, and instinctively she drew back with a cry.

'It's safely moored,' Hervé assured her. 'We have only to wait until the tide's just past the turn, and then climb down. It's not far, and I have a ladder. I made sure of that.'

Kate felt sick; and leant weakly back

against the wall.

'I can't,' she whispered, the words lost in the tumult. If Hervé sensed her fear he did not show it. He grasped her arm and pulled her back to where she could look down again on the sea.

'We must watch for the right moment,' he said.

They stood there for what seemed like hours to Kate, as her sense of disbelieving panic grew and grew, and she wondered if she would be overcome by hysteria before Hervé gave the signal that the time had come. 'I *must* trust him – I *must!*' she told herself, but the words repeated themselves meaninglessly in her head, failing completely to reach her terror-stricken spirit. It was almost a relief when the hand on her arm gave a sharp tug, and Hervé growled: 'Now!' He pulled a bundle from beneath his arm, secured one end somehow to the parapet, and flung the other over. A rope ladder snaked its way down the wall into the dark.

He made her go first. 'It's safer that way,' he assured her, though she could not see how. Shaking so much that she wondered if she would be able to hold on to the ladder, she climbed with his help on to the parapet and then lowered herself very slowly on to the swaying rungs at the far side. She shut her eyes. Anything was better than to risk a glimpse of that boiling cauldron of a sea below.

Very slowly she edged her way down, feeling each rung with nervous feet. At one point one of her shoes fell off, but on the whole it was easier to feel her way without them; and in any case she knew she would never find it again. After a moment or two she felt the ladder shudder as Hervé lowered himself on to it above her head.

She came to a halt at last, swaying sickeningly over the water, and clutched tight in terror as a wave swept over her and shot a great spout of water up the wall nearby. It receded, leaving her drenched and shivering and sobbing with cold and fear.

'Jump!' shouted Hervé. 'Now, at once!'

She opened her eyes and could just make out, rocking drunkenly, the little boat, close at hand. But the short stretch of water between herself and it seemed limitless, stretching to infinity. 'I can't!' she moaned, knowing Hervé could not hear. She felt his foot prod her shoulder. 'Jump,' he shouted again, moving one rung lower so that she had to lean back over the sea to give him room.

She had no choice, so she gathered all her

strength, and jumped. She landed awkwardly, one hand clasping the side of the boat, her body sprawled half over the edge, so that the vessel tilted dangerously, almost overturned. The next moment it shot the other way as Hervé leapt neatly across her and righted the balance. Then he dragged her in after him. She lay huddled in the bottom, her face hidden, shivering uncontrollably, while Hervé took the oars, until now lashed to the inside of the boat, and, choosing his moment with care, cut the mooring rope and began skilfully to row them away from the angry power of the breaking waves.

Out beyond the rocks the sea was astonishingly quiet and calm, and the boat rose and fell gently over the waves. Hervé took them in a wide circle about the city and then turned into the river estuary, making his way steadily inland and upstream.

Slowly Kate began to regain control of herself. An intense desire not to show her weakness before Hervé gave her courage, and she raised her head and sat up and tried to look as though she was as cool and untroubled as he appeared to be. But she could not control the shivering which shook her incessantly, and she knew she must look white and drawn from the horror of that escape. She had to set her face in hard lines and hold herself very stiffly to give any kind of impression of calmness. She knew that a very little would make her break down altogether.

Fortunately Hervé did not seem to be in a talkative mood. Perhaps he had been more alarmed himself by the risks he had taken than his appearance suggested. As it was, he scarcely looked at Kate, and said nothing at all until he brought the boat to rest against the river bank about two miles inland from St Malo. Then he gave a jerk of his head.

'Out!' he commanded. 'We walk now.'

The evening's experiences seemed to have temporarily deprived Kate of the sympathetic ally of the past days. Clearly, thought Kate, Hervé had indeed been more afraid tonight than he had seemed. It made her feel less uncomfortable about her own cowardly performance. At least surely the worst must be over now.

She stepped on to the shore, mortified to find how weak and unsteady her legs felt as she put her weight on to them. She stumbled and almost fell, and had to reach out to a nearby tree trunk for support.

'Where do we go now?' she asked Hervé,

as cheerfully as she could, trying to cover her shameful inadequacy. Hervé clapped a hand over her mouth.

'Quiet!' he hissed in her ear. 'Just follow me!'

She followed, obediently if painfully, because of her now bare feet, along a narrow overgrown path through a small wood, where only her companion's hand on her wrist gave her any guidance. After that, they followed a rutted road for some distance, and then crossed fields and more woods and another road, and came at dawn within sight of a village. Hervé laid a hand on Kate's arm.

'Wait here,' he ordered, pulling her into the concealment of some trees. And then he disappeared from view.

He reappeared after a moment of two with a battered cart pulled by an overworked-looking horse, and told her to climb up. She did so, thankful to rest her sore feet, and he urged the horse forward. She did not ask how he had come by the vehicle. She strongly suspected it was stolen, in which case it was better not to know.

They made progress more quickly after that, though Kate could still gain no reply to her repeated enquiries as to where they were going. Hervé clearly regarded such questions as trivial conversation, to be avoided. He spoke only when it was essential to do so, his manner abrupt, almost morose. Kate began after some hours to feel just a little uneasy, but after all he, like her, must by now be exhausted, and some shortness of temper was thus excusable.

Some time in the afternoon he found them some bread to eat – again she did not ask how he had come by it – and then pulled the cart deep into a wood and told her to take the opportunity to sleep, as he was going to do. They would go on their way after dark. Kate fell asleep almost at once, so exhausted was she, but slept for only a short time, waking cold and stiff and shot by sudden panic a little before it grew dark. Her nerves seemed to have been shattered by all that had happened, for there was no reason for panic. The wood was quiet, but for the gentle evening sounds of birds settling down to roost for the night, and small animals scuttling though the undergrowth; and the horse cropping the grass; and Hervé's rhythmic snoring. Kate stretched, and jumped down from the cart and walked about for a little to warm herself, thankful for the tranquillity of the place. It seemed very far removed from the wild tumult of the waves against the city walls, though she wondered if anything would ever drive out their lingering sound in her ears.

She wandered some distance from the cart, and stood in a clearing not far from the fringe of the wood, and watched the sun setting in molten gold behind the dark tracery of the trees. The peace of it all had scarcely had time to reach her before Hervé came with a crash along the path behind her and seized her arm.

'Where are you going?'

She looked round, astonished at the scowling anger of his face.

'I was just walking,' she explained mildly.

'We must go now,' he said, not releasing her. He dragged her back with him towards the cart, and thrust her roughly against it. 'Get up.'

She did so, her uneasiness reviving sharply. She watched him as well as she could in the dim light as he scrambled on to the cart and took the reins in his hand. His expression was stony and withdrawn. She wanted to ask him what was wrong, and what he had been afraid of when he woke to find her gone, but she dared not. In any case, he had taken an enormous risk in helping her to escape. She ought to be grateful, and trust that he would not let her down now.

They came next evening, after another wearying and silent day, to a small stone house, sheltered by trees and set in well cared-for farmland. As they approached, two dogs came running barking towards them, and Hervé reined in the horse and gave a great shout. A man came to the door, stared for a moment, and called off the dogs; and then set out at a run, followed by a large woman panting behind him.

Bewildered, Kate watched Hervé jump from the cart to be enveloped in repeated embraces and swept by a flood of emotional greetings. Two other men came from further afield, and the welcome began all over again. It was clear at least that Hervé had brought her to some kinsfolk of his.

Eventually, he seemed to remember her existence. He pulled her unceremoniously down to stand beside him and made a perfunctory introduction which explained nothing of her reasons for being there. However, Kate saw a glance travel between him and the woman, and guessed that he intended to say more later, when she was not there to hear. It did not make her feel any more at ease. After that he said to her curtly: 'My mother – my brothers,' and she smiled faintly at the staring faces. Then he took her arm and led her inside, followed by the brothers laughing and talking. They went along a stone-flagged passage, through a low doorway, and to another door at the far side of what was clearly the dairy. And then Kate found herself pushed into near-darkness and heard behind her the unmistakable sound of a door being closed and bolted.

Rage set her alight. She turned and ran to the door and hammered fiercely on it with her fists.

'Let me out! Let me out this instant! How dare you! Hervé! Hervé!'

A laugh, faint and distant, reached her, and then silence.

She shouted until she was exhausted, and then the anger drained from her, leaving her cold and very frightened. What had she done when she had turned for help to Hervé? Why had he brought her here? What did he mean to do with her? All at once she found herself in a situation to which there were no answers, and she was horribly afraid. She had no idea what was going to happen to her. She had not been so frightened since her first night of captivity on board the *Marguerite,* and in some ways this was even worse, perhaps because she knew that she had brought it on herself. It seemed interminably long until a faint light outlined the door and seeped into the room, and told her that morning had come.

Some time after the dawn Hervé brought her a breakfast of bread and milk, placing the wooden plate and beaker on the floor without a word, and turning at once to go. Hiding her fear, Kate caught at his arm.

'Hervé – what's happened? What about the boat to take me to England?'

He smiled, and she wondered how she could ever have thought him sympathetic.

'There'll be a boat, when we're ready,' he said, and shook off her hand and went out, bolting the door again behind him. Kate sank helplessly down on the floor and stared at the closed door and cursed herself for being a gullible fool. She cursed Tristan de Plouvinel too, for being so overwhelmingly attractive that the heartache of loving him without hope had driven her to this. But she knew that was not very fair. She had only herself to blame in the end.

That evening Hervé and his brothers must have been in celebratory mood, for the sound of their laughter and singing reached even to this remote corner of the house. After some time, it began to come nearer, and she heard the unmistakable sounds of approaching feet,

133

and the door was flung open. Hervé, very drunk, half fell inside, and then reached out and pulled her to him. What he said next she did not understand, for it was slurred by drink and very colloquial, and the laughing remarks of his brothers behind him were equally incomprehensible; but of his intensions there could be no doubt. He held her against him, his hands pawing her eagerly, his panting breath hot on her face. She struggled fiercely, but his grasp only tightened, and he pushed her against the wall. She felt swept by a wave of disbelieving horror as one dirty sweating hand made its way inside the neck of her gown and down to her breast. She struggled wildly, biting and kicking, but he had her pinned too tight against the wall for escape. She could hear the brothers laughing and shouting encouragement behind him. It was a nightmare, but it was real.

And then a fiercely commanding voice broke in, Hervé's hands stilled; and then he drew back and thrust her from him. She fell awkwardly, striking her head on the wall, and sat rubbing her bruised scalp and staring at the angrily gesticulating figure of Hervé's mother, who was perhaps no friend of hers but had saved her from an ugly fate. For that she had her gratitude.

A little after, Hervé lurched sullenly away and the door was slammed shut and bolted. Kate stayed where she was, gazing at it in despairing gloom. Whatever prospect lay before her now, she knew it was at the best a cheerless one. She doubted if she would ever see England, or William, or her family again. She wished only that this nightmare might soon come to an end, however horrible that end might be.

The night passed slowly, with little sleep and no comfort. She was weak with hunger, for Hervé seemed to have forgotten that she must eat, and the bread and milk of her last breakfast had not been enough to sustain her for so long as this. She had not eaten very much during the previous days either. But she knew she had only herself to blame for her present plight. Oddly, it kept her spirits up a little to be so angry with herself.

But by morning they had fallen to their lowest point. Beyond the tiny window a grey dawn brought rain, torrential rain whose noise shut out all other sounds. It seemed to rain endlessly, for hours. No one brought her anything to eat, and no steps approached her prison – though at that she was rather re-lieved. She feared another visit from Hervé like that of last night. Next time his mother might not be on hand to rescue her.

At one point during the morning she thought she could make out, above the drumming of the rain, a confused noise of shouting, but she was not sure if it was real or imagined. She hoped fervently that Hervé was not drinking again.

Then, a little later, she knew without any doubt at all that someone was running across the dairy towards her prison. She heard a brief shouted exchange – she knew Hervé had a part in it – and she rose to her feet and shrank back against the wall, bracing herself against it as the bolts shot free and the door was flung wide.

Hervé pulled her roughly to him, but this time it was not his appetite but his safety which was at stake. He swung her round until she stood in front of him, held in a harsh ferocious grip; and so brought her face to face with his pursuer, towering in the doorway, coming there to a sudden shocked halt. Tristan de Plouvinel's eyes met hers, angry and at the same time wary, as if he dared not make any move for fear he startled Hervé into some fatal action. The seaman had a long knife in his hand, and its blade lay gleaming evilly against Kate's throat.

'Get out, or she'll die!' Hervé warned sharply.

Tristan's hand, holding his sword, relaxed against his side, though with a visible effort of will. Kate felt no matching relaxation in the tensed figure behind her. The hand twisting her arms behind her was ruthless in its grasp, and she felt the knife blade move on her throat, and shut her eyes in momentary terror.

'Don't be a fool, Hervé. This will do you no good.' Tristan's voice sounded amazingly calm, like any reasonable man discussing some minor point of interest with another. 'Doesn't he care?' thought Kate. 'Doesn't he realise what danger I'm in?' She opened her eyes again and looked at him, and saw by the hard line of his jaw, the alert gleam of his eyes that the quiet manner was deceptive. She wanted to cry out 'Help me!', but she dared not, for fear she would startle Hervé into using the knife. And what could Tristan do, that would not be fatal to her?

'Put that sword away!' ordered Hervé. 'Otherwise I'll use this knife, and you'll not get your ransom.'

'Nor, may I remind you, will you have your share,' Tristan pointed out; but he sheathed the sword obediently.

Hervé spat, with a precision born of long practice, and Kate felt the knife quiver.

'*That's* for my share!' he said. 'But much you care, so long as you can line your pockets from the sweat of our brows.'

Tristan raised an eyebrow.

'So you feel hard done by? You've kept that very quiet. After all, the prizes have always been divided up by agreement – agreement in which you have as much say as anyone – more than most, in fact, for you've always had a generous portion. I can think of no other man in your position who's done as well.'

'That's it, isn't it? "In my position". Second in command, always. There you are, the fine nobleman with all his airs and graces. Never mind that you come from a rotting little manor house with holes in the roof, never mind that you started with nothing but debts, while my people with honest hard work kept the roof sound over our heads and bread in our bellies without help from you – and paid our rents to you, on time and in full, for you and yours to gamble away at court. But of course we didn't have fine ladies taking a fancy to us – old enough to be your mother, too, isn't she? How does that feel, letting her bed you?' Tristan made a sudden movement, stilled almost at once, though only with great difficulty. 'So there you were, all set for a fine time at sea – and who did the work, to pay for a new roof on your manor and horses for your coach, and fine clothes for court dress? Friend Hervé again, of course. That's my position, isn't it – second in command, and last in line for the rewards that are going? Well, I tell you now that's going to change. If there's any money coming in for this girl, I'm having it–'

'Then you'd better let her go hadn't you?' suggested Tristan pleasantly. 'They may not be prepared to pay for a corpse. I shouldn't.'

'When you leave my house, I'll let her go.'

'And what does your mother say to that? She at least was always loyal – and your brother André?'

'André knows what's good for him – and my mother's an old fool. She'd come running at the bidding of any de Plouvinel, no matter what they asked of her.'

'Because my mother was her friend – and I mean friend: to her there was no inequality. But I can't expect you to understand friendship, or loyalty. Once I thought you did, but I know better now. You knew I'd find out what you'd been up to, didn't you? That's why you took such a risk getting

139

away from St Malo – Miss Pendleton was just an incidental–' With apparent ease, he relaxed still further, leaning against the door. He looked almost bored. 'How long do you intend to stay there like that, Hervé? Doesn't it make your arm ache?'

'Not much longer, Monsieur le Capitaine. Five more minutes and if you're not gone there'll be an ugly red mark on this pretty white throat–'

'Your mother won't like it,' commented Tristan. Kate heard Hervé swear softly, jolting with irritation. What was Tristan doing? If he went on like this Hervé would kill her on impulse, or even by accident.

'Go on – get out!' her captor repeated.

Tristan was not even looking at them now. He was yawning, his eyes almost closed, as if the whole situation wearied him. Then he shifted his position slightly and stood gazing down at the floor, whistling a little tune between his teeth.

It seemed a long time that they waited there like that, Hervé holding her, the knife at her throat, Tristan apparently paying almost no attention to them. And then, all at once without a hint of a warning he sprang forward. Kate felt Hervé's grasp tighten, but at the same instant the knife was snatched free of her throat and fell clattering to the floor, and she was flung aside while the two men grappled together, struggling noisily in the tiny space. Kate ran into the dairy, and looked on in shivering horror.

A moment or two after, Hervé was crouched in the corner and Tristan stood over him, sword in hand. Kate shuddered, waiting for the final blow, her eyes on the cowering figure of Hervé, his face ashen.

But the blow did not come. Instead Tristan said: 'For the friendship that was between our mothers, I shall spare you. Remember that, Hervé, and learn from it. For be quite sure that if you cross my path ever again I shall not be so generous. I shall lock you in now, and when we have left your mother may let you out, in her own time.'

He backed out of the cell, pushed the bolts home, and sheathed his sword; and then he turned to look frowningly at Kate. Slowly, she came towards him, her legs trembling wildly, sick with reaction. Oh, for those arms to fold about her and hold her close, shutting out the nightmare of the past days, telling her as no words could that she was safe and no harm could come to her ever again!

But instead his hands closed about her

elbows, holding her steady a little distance away from him, and his eyes, grave and dark, ran over her.

'Are you hurt?' he asked abruptly. He was still frowning, but she could not believe that his anger was directed at her.

'I'm all right,' she replied. If he had held her she would have wept, and cried out her relief and thanks and gratitude; but his own restraint seemed to affect her, and she became awkward, not quite knowing what to say or how to behave.

'Let's get away from here then,' he said; and, turning, led her across the dairy, and along the passage to the front door. The rain had ceased by now. Out in the yard Hervé's mother was scattering grain to the hens, but she turned to meet them, her eyes anxious. Tristan gave her a brief explanation, and kissed her, and her thanks followed them as he led Kate to his waiting horse.

Kate glanced up at him as they walked, wanting herself to say how grateful she was that he had come after her. Indoors, his frowning abruptness had put her off, but now he had spoken so gently to Hervé's mother she felt he must be more ready to listen kindly to her. But she knew at once that she had misjudged the situation. That look of glowering anger had settled again over his face, and she dared not speak.

The horse was a massive beast, but muddied and travel-stained as was Tristan himself, and clearly weary. With as few words as possible Tristan helped Kate to mount, and then gathered the reins into his hands and led the animal forward. Kate noticed for the first time, with sudden sharp anxiety, that he was limping badly.

'You should be riding!' she said quickly.

'We have not far to go,' he returned. 'And this horse has been working too hard already to bear two riders. Besides, my leg will be better for the walk. I have sat too long in the saddle these past days.'

'You shouldn't have done so much so soon after you were hurt,' she reproached him. 'It can't be good for you.'

'Perhaps you should have thought of that before putting yourself in Hervé's hands.'

'I didn't know he was like that.'

'Perhaps not – but you had no reason to run away, had you? Were you not treated with every kindness?'

'I was still your prisoner,' she reminded him, her voice sharp with indignation; and then, remembering what had driven her to that reckless flight, she coloured faintly. She could never tell him the truth, that she had gone because to have him near her, as he was now, was more than she could bear. Looking back, she thought how foolish she had been. She would be thankful in future for every moment that they could be together, and not trouble any longer about what tomorrow might bring.

'You had only to wait, and you would have been free.'

'Yes,' she said meekly. 'I'm sorry.'

He said no more, relapsing into a thoughtful silence. He looked tired, Kate thought; but if he had ridden after her from St Malo, resting little on the way, he would be tired. And he must have ridden hard, to find her so soon.

'How did you know I would be here,' she asked.

'I guessed.'

'When did you leave St Malo?'

'Two nights ago, as soon as I knew you had gone.'

He must have ridden without a break, or he would hardly be here now. And with that long ride added to his recent illness he must, Kate realised with a pang of compunction, be close to exhaustion. It was no wonder if weariness made him taciturn, unwilling to talk. After all, she too was tired, exhausted by the terrors of this escape which had gone so badly wrong and turned out to be no kind of escape at all. She wondered, without any great interest, where he was taking her now, being thankful only that he had assured her it was not far.

The next moment they were there, in a weed-grown stable yard beside an old stone house, gently turreted, as if it were reminding the observer that it was more than a mere farmhouse, but was all the same first and foremost a home. Hens scratched over the yard amongst the pigeons which flew clamorously up as the horse approached. An elderly woman emerged into the watery sunshine, drying her hands on her apron.

Tristan greeted her warmly in some unknown lilting language which Kate supposed must be Breton, and then turned to lift Kate down from the saddle. She felt his hands on her waist, steadying her, strong and warm, and then, suddenly overcome with dizziness, she sank against him.

She was confusedly aware then that he lifted her into his arms and carried her quickly indoors. She heard hurrying feet, doors opening, knew she had been lowered on to a bed, blessedly soft and yielding to her weary body. Low voices talked somewhere above her, and then steps receded, and a door closed. A woman's voice, gentle and soothing, murmured over her, and pulled the covers about her, and brought her warm milk to drink. And then, safe at last, she fell asleep.

Nine

Kate did not stir until the early sunlight of the following day crossed the worn polished boards of the floor and reached the curtained bed where she lay. Only then, slowly and cautiously, did she open her eyes.

She had feared for a brief but horrible moment that she would find herself still in the cold cell in Hervé's house. But the softness of the bed beneath her relaxed body, the warmth that enfolded her, the sense of space and of peace told her even before she opened her eyes that she was safe. Safe at least from that particular horror.

She did remember though with a twinge of apprehension that Tristan's mood yesterday had been less than warm. The laughing friendliness had gone from his manner, and she did not like the frowning displeasure which seemed to have replaced it. He had rescued her, of course, and that suggested some kind of concern for her, but then she was to be the means of making a large sum of money for him. He would not readily lose

147

that opportunity. She had the feeling too that he had been hurt by her flight, as if it reflected in some way on his care of her. But perhaps, she thought now, she was reading too much into his behaviour yesterday. If nothing else he must have been very tired. This morning, after a night's rest, it would all be different.

Indeed Kate herself felt enormously refreshed by her own sound, untroubled sleep. She stretched luxuriously, and then slid from the bed and crossed to the window. Below, an overgrown garden spread green and disorderly to a sheltering wood, reminding her for a moment with what was almost a pang of regret of the little garden at St Malo. Though this was very much larger, with signs here and there that it had once been laid out and tended with elaborate care.

There was no sign of human activity anywhere, except that someone downstairs was singing and clattering pots. Kate became sharply aware that she was extremely hungry, and hurried to pull on her now thoroughly disreputable clothes and go in search of some kind of breakfast. Fortunately, someone had left a pair of battered shoes at her bedside, near her other garments, clearly intended for her. They did not fit very well, but they were better than nothing, and she put them on.

She followed the distant sounds along a passage and down a wide flight of stairs, across a stone-flagged dimly lit hall and into a cavernous kitchen in which the elderly woman she remembered from last night was working busily.

It was only a very short time after that before Kate found herself seated at a scrubbed table eating hungrily while the old woman chattered away in a confusing mixture of Breton and broken French, and seemed not to mind that Kate merely murmured uncomprehending agreement from time to time. One fact only Kate gleaned from the cheerful flood of talk, and that was that Monsieur le Comte was still in bed.

Her hunger satisfied, Kate sat quietly for some time watching the old woman at work, and thinking that she had until now assumed that this house belonged to her present companion, and that she must be some old acquaintance of Tristan's. But she remembered how yesterday Tristan had spoken of the old friendship between his mother and Hervé's. Did that mean that they were near neighbours? And could it be then that he had brought her to his own family home?

She doubted her own ability to make the old woman understand what she wanted to know, and instead decided to set out on a tour of exploration. Perhaps she could answer the question for herself.

Now that she had eaten she was better able to take in her surroundings. She was struck this time by the generally uncared-for look of the old house, the dust filming the heavily carved furniture, the worn hangings, the empty hearths in which the ashes had long been cold. Yet there was something both homely and welcoming about the low-ceilinged rooms, the wide windows lit by a green light from the trees crowding beyond them. It might be old-fashioned and neglected, but with care this house could be turned into the lovely place it must once have been.

In a wide parlour Kate found one of the clues she had been seeking: a group of family portraits gazing down on the dust and neglect. There was a tall darkly handsome man in the full splendour of military dress of about fifty years ago: something in his eyes, bright, alert, eager, brought Tristan to mind. There was a slender brown-haired young woman, whose blue silk gown echoed the blue of her eyes. And there was an enchanting family group, in which the same couple stood with joined hands and reached with tender gestures towards a laughing black-eyed boy who played at their feet with a fat puppy. She had no doubt now who the boy was, and beneath whose roof his portrait hung.

A little later she wandered out into the garden, shining in the sun after yesterday's rain. There were roses half-choked with weeds, herbs in overgrown confusion, an apple orchard whose long grass was tangled with brambles. There was a statue of a cupid with a broken arm, and a stone bench so hidden by weeds that she almost fell over it before she knew it was there. It was moss-grown and very damp, or she would have sat down on it, for it offered a good vantage point from which to observe the house. She was standing looking down on it, frowning slightly, when a voice speaking suddenly behind her sent her spinning round in alarm.

'I know exactly of what you are thinking,' it said. Kate stood glaring up at him, one hand to her heaving breast, and gasped out: 'You made me jump!'

Tristan gave a little bow, and she was

cheered to see that the old mocking sparkle was back in his eyes.

'My apologies, Miss Kate.' Then he added: 'But am I not right? Are you not considering how you would like at once to work in this garden?'

Kate laughed. 'Yes,' she admitted. 'It's in a shocking state, you must agree. Does it belong to you too?'

'As you see, I am no gardener,' he said by way of reply. 'I send money to my steward, but that is for the estate. I rarely come here, so there is no one to care what becomes of the garden or of the house.'

'That's a pity. It could be lovely.'

'I think you are right. Perhaps one day it will be different– Did you sleep well beneath my roof?'

As she assured him that she had, Kate studied him. He did not look as if he, for his part, had found the night as refreshing as she had. His face had a grey drawn look, which troubled her; and she noticed that he was leaning rather too heavily on the pedestal of the broken cupid, as if he felt the need for its support.

'I had thought,' he said after a moment, 'that we should go on our way today–'

'I don't think you're fit to ride!' she burst

out. He smiled faintly.

'I had no intention of riding. There is a coach in the stables, and adequate horses– But in any case I think you should rest a little more today, and then you will be ready to travel tomorrow.'

Kate accepted his estimate of her own needs without comment. If it helped his pride to pretend that it was she who required a rest, then she was not the one to argue with that; so long as he did not continue to over-exert himself.

'I'm happy to stay here as long as you wish,' she said meekly, and truthfully.

'One day will be enough – more than enough, for I must be ready to go to sea again at the end of next week.'

'That shouldn't be a problem – it won't take more than two or three days to reach St Malo, will it?'

'We are not going to St Malo,' he pointed out, with a hint of dryness. 'I am taking you to St Germain.'

Kate stared at him.

'St Germain! But why?'

'It seems that your brother is there – and the King commands it. So you see if you had waited you would in any case have been free of me. You will be glad, will you not?'

Will I? thought Kate, her eyes held by his. She could not take it all in, less still know whether she was glad or not. She thought first; 'So Harry *is* at St Germain,' and then she felt a sudden searing disappointment at the knowledge that she would never again sit in that now familiar room and play at cards with her captor, or linger over supper in his company. When that knowledge reached her, she bit her lip and bent her head so that he should not read her feelings in her face.

There was a pause, and then he said: 'What entertainment may I offer you?'

Kate looked up at him, aware only too well that he must want most of all to retire to his own room and recover his strength for tomorrow's journey. He would not wish to put any more strain on his leg, if he was hoping to go to sea again next week.

'I can entertain myself very well, thank you,' she said politely. 'If you don't mind me wandering about as I please, that is.'

She was not sure, watching him, whether he was relieved or offended at her independence. She thought she could read both emotions at once in his expression; but when he spoke he sounded simply detached and courteous. 'As you wish. I shall leave you, then, to your own devices.'

She stood watching as he limped away from her across the garden towards the house, and then all at once sank down on the seat, heedless of its dampness.

So the command of the King had transformed her in a moment from a prisoner to an honoured guest! There was to be no ransom. She was free; she would see Harry again; she need not yet go to Ireland, and William, and marriage, for this gave her a breathing space. She should, she knew, feel both grateful and happy at the prospect before her.

Yet here she was shot through with regret that she had at the most only a few more days of Tristan's company before her, and not the weeks or even months for which she had hoped. Love, she reflected ruefully, made one amazingly changeable and illogical. Had she not run away from St Malo for just that reason, because she could not any longer bear the pain of Tristan's company? And now that she was to be freed from it, she found herself wishing only to bind herself again.

'You're a fool!' she told herself firmly, and stood up and began to walk about the garden, trying to bring herself to a more sensible frame of mind.

After all, she acknowledged that if this prospect had been offered to her just a few short weeks ago, before she found herself Tristan's prisoner, then she would have been delighted. She would have rejoiced at seeing Harry again, at being able to stay at the court of the exiled King James, at the thought of all the excitements awaiting her in this foreign land. She would have recognised that life held out to her the promise of enjoyment, adventure and new experiences.

But now she had met Tristan de Plouvinel and knew that she wanted nothing more from life than to spend every hour left to her in his company.

Only, she knew too that her dream could never be realised. Whether she had months or weeks or days left in Tristan's company, they must come to an end, and she must then learn to go on alone, and accept the heartache and the sense of loss, and make what she could of life without him. At least at St Germain with her beloved brother it was likely to be easier for her. The court must offer diversions of all kinds to distract a heartbroken girl from her unhappiness, and Harry had always been the most loving and understanding of companions. Of course, that would only be a way of putting off a little the inevitable marriage to William. After all, the marriage contract was drawn up, her grandfather's dowry ready to be paid, and all that was needed was for her to arrive in Ireland to make those final and irrevocable vows. If William had paid her ransom, and she had been returned to him, then the marriage – already delayed – would have taken place at once. As it was, she now had the opportunity of a little time to herself, to recover from the experiences of the past weeks and prepare herself somehow, if it was possible, for the long dreary years of wedlock. She should, she knew, be grateful for that.

She had even convinced herself that she was grateful, and brought herself to a calmer frame of mind, by the time the old woman came to summon her to dinner. She ate, as before, in the kitchen: Monsieur le Comte, she was told, was eating alone in his room. Since she had wanted him to rest she could hardly complain at that, but she could not help wishing that she could be with him now. There was so little time left, and it was passing so quickly.

After dinner she explored a little further

afield, through the stable yard and the grouped farm buildings and into the woods and meadows beyond. It was a gentle countryside, level and tranquil and wooded. But she noted with disapproval how many of the buildings were in need of repair, and how neglected the fields looked. Everywhere there was the same uncared-for aspect that she had found in the house and the garden. She wondered if Tristan ever troubled to find out what his steward was doing in his absence. Perhaps she would mention it to him when she saw him again.

But she did not see him any more that day. After supper she talked for a while, with difficulty but with enjoyment, to the old servant, who remembered Tristan as a boy and had many tales to tell of his escapades. Then, as it grew dark, she made her way to bed. She passed the door of Tristan's room as she went: she knew which it was, for she had seen the old woman come from there with an empty tray earlier in the day. Now there was no rim of light around the door. He must have gone to sleep.

She lay for a long while in bed listening to the sound of the wind in the trees outside and thinking of all that had happened to her, and all that might yet happen. And trying not to remember the moments which had been so sweet and yet held such pain for her now when she thought of them. She must try and forget, just a little, if she was ever going to find any kind of happiness again.

She felt at last that she had been awake for hours, and yet still sleep eluded her. She had left the shutters open, and the moonlight stretched across the floor, almost as bright as day except that the shadows in contrast were so densely black. Eventually, she got out of bed and went to look out on the moonlit garden.

Its neglected state was invisible now in the night, and it looked only beautiful, all silvered and shadowed in the cold light. The wind had dropped, and it was quite still, quiet but for the hooting of an owl from some way off. A dark shape – a deer, perhaps, for it was too big for a fox or a cat – slipped out from the shadow of the wood and crossed the path towards the house.

Only it was not a deer, she realised, but a man.

Kate drew one sharp shocked breath, and stepped back into the concealment of the folded shutters. What man would be likely to be walking in the garden at this time of night? It was not Tristan, for he was too short and slight for that, and surely no one else ought to be out there at this time?

Suddenly chilled with fear she turned and ran softly from the room and along the passage, and pushed open Tristan's door.

He lay on his side, facing her, in a canopied bed with the curtains drawn back; and he was fast asleep. But some hard-learned instinct must have been at work, for she had taken only two steps into the room before she saw his eyes gleam in the dark, and knew he was watching her.

He sat up. 'Miss Kate!' he whispered in astonishment. 'What are you doing here?'

She felt all at once very foolish. Now that she was not alone she began to think she must have imagined it all. In any case, even if she had not there was probably some perfectly reasonable explanation. She had very likely woken Tristan for nothing.

'I...,' she began. 'I thought I saw ... I'm not sure ... only I think there was a man in the garden.'

'Mon Dieu!' Tristan exclaimed with a despairing gesture of the hands. 'You wake me for that? Did you not suffer perhaps a nightmare?'

Kate shook her head firmly.

'I've not been to sleep,' she said.

Tristan sighed, and climbed resignedly out of bed and went to the window. It looked out on the same portion of garden as did hers, but now all was quiet, still and untroubled in the moonlight.

'There – are you satisfied?' demanded Tristan, turning to look at her. And then he drew in his breath and stood quite still. It was at that moment that Kate realised that she had burst at night into a man's bedroom dressed only in her shift. And that this was the man who, once, had lost control of himself in her company. She began to shiver, but not with cold. The room was very quiet, and she could hear his quickened breathing, and her own in response. She felt his eyes run over her, and knew the lines of her body were only too visible through the thin fabric. He wore little enough himself: a loose ruffled shirt, beneath which his strong legs and feet were bare. He was so near, he had only to reach out a hand to touch her – and she wanted it, wanted it more than anything, now, at this moment–

'I want–' she found herself whispering. 'I want–' and then she broke off and thought: 'What am I doing?'

She never knew what might have happened next, for he did reach out his hand to touch her, and her whole instinct was to move in response to that gesture closer to the hard muscular body, the strong arms, the hands that once had caressed her– And then, all at once, a sudden sharp sound from below made them both turn quickly back to the window.

The garden looked exactly as it had before, but there could be no doubt about the sound, as of a foot striking metal perhaps. The sound a man might make stumbling over some hidden obstacle in the dark. And it came from immediately below the window, where the shadows were deep about a rampant climbing rose. Kate felt Tristan's arm close about her shoulder, drawing her near as if in reassurance and protection. She was caught dizzyingly between fear and delight, though the delight was uppermost, for how could she be afraid with him so near, the hard lines of his body against hers, his arm warm about her shoulder? She had only to turn her head just a very little, reach up, and her mouth would find his–

Only that alluring mouth was closed in a firm line, and the brows drawn together with concentration, and his attention was quite clearly on the disturbance below, and not at all on his companion. Probably that protective gesture had been purely instinctive. Very likely he did not even know he had done it. Kate tried to return her wandering thoughts to the possible intruder. Earlier tonight, on first glimpsing him, an alarming possibility had occurred to her.

'Could it be Hervé?' she whispered now. 'If his mother had let him go–?'

Tristan glanced at her briefly, and let his arm fall, and drew away from her, his expression remote and preoccupied.

'It is possible. I shall not allow it to trouble me.' He moved as if to return to bed, and Kate gave a soft cry.

'You can't just ignore it!' she protested. 'You know how he hates you. What if he wants revenge?'

Tristan shrugged.

'He knows what I shall do to him if he tries to take revenge. That is up to him.'

'But there is no one in the house apart from you and me and the old lady downstairs. What if he breaks in while we are asleep?'

She could not be sure, but she thought Tristan looked faintly amused.

'Do you think me unable to protect myself?'

'If you were asleep–' She remembered how he had woken at her first soft footfall at his bedside. But could he always be sure of waking so easily?

She felt his hand, warm and a little rough to the touch, slide beneath her chin, tilting her head so that he could look directly into her face.

'You must not be afraid. I shall let no harm come to you, or to myself, or to anyone else. The house is well secured downstairs. Go back to your bed. Close your shutters and lock your door. You will be safe, I promise. And I, I shall do the same.' His hand fell, and Kate, disappointed, stood gazing at him, not moving. 'Go – there is nothing to fear,' he said a little impatiently, and one glance at his abstracted frown sent her scuttling meekly from the room.

She closed the shutters and bolted the door, but she did not go to bed. Instead she sat for a long time on its edge straining her ears for any unusual sound. She heard, with some small relief, the unmistakable clatter of Tristan's shutters closing, and his own door being bolted, but even that could not reassure her. All the dreadful experiences of the past days came flooding back into her mind, driving out the calmness which a quiet day in Tristan's home had brought. She remembered Hervé urging her into the wave-tossed boat, remembered him flinging her into the little cell, remembered how he had come drunkenly to fumble his way over her body, and worst of all the knife at her throat and the hate-filled voice in her ear. All that, not from any malice towards her, but to wreak some kind of vengeance on a man he had envied and hated for years. A man who, with an almost sentimental generosity, had let him go free though he had Hervé at his mercy. Would that generosity be enough to stir Hervé's conscience, and make him mend his ways? Kate doubted it, and she guessed that Tristan too thought it was unlikely. Or had he merely been humouring her when he took her fear seriously tonight? She did not know; but it was a very long time until the chill of the night drove her into bed at last, and even longer before she fell finally into a fitful sleep.

Ten

Early next morning Tristan joined Kate for breakfast looking as if he had never been tired or ill, and certainly quite unlike a man whose sleep had been disturbed. His cool brisk manner irritated Kate, who had no such immunity to the effects of sleeplessness. But then, she thought sourly, perhaps he had found no difficulty in sleeping once she had left him. It was only she who had been kept wakeful by the danger that threatened him.

Unless of course he had indeed failed to take her seriously, as she had thought possible last night. When the thanks were said, and the final leave-takings, and they were seated side by side in the heavy old-fashioned and not very comfortable coach which was to take them on their way, Kate asked bluntly: 'Did you believe me when I said there was someone in the garden last night? Did you really think it might be Hervé?' Even she, in daylight, wondered if she had been frightened without cause.

Tristan shrugged.

'It is possible. I do not know. But today we leave him behind. He will not follow, I think. He knows better than that.'

He fell silent, dismissing the subject, and turned to look out of the window. Kate watched him, her heart sinking at the grimness of his expression. Yesterday's lighter mood had gone, and they were back to that of the day before. She felt depressed. Their last days together must not be like this, marked by coldness and constraint.

Beyond Tristan's strong profile, Kate glimpsed the passing countryside, the fields and woods and the little clustered cottages. That reminded her of something, distracting her from other troubles.

'When I was out walking yesterday,' she told him, 'I saw that many of the buildings looked in need of repair. I am no expert, of course. But are you sure you can trust your steward if you are here so little?' Even as she spoke, she wished the words unsaid. 'Why do I have to be so outspoken?' she thought with dismay. 'After all, it's none of my business.'

He turned to look at her with an expression of such astonishment that she braced herself for his anger. But to her surprise his face relaxed into a slight wry smile, and he said only: 'Be assured, Miss Kate, that I intend to make a longer visit before too long. If there are faults, I shall rectify them. Does that satisfy your desire for order?'

Kate blushed and nodded. 'Yes,' she said faintly, relieved that she had been let off so lightly. She was disappointed though that his smile faded quickly afterwards, and silence fell like a heavy curtain between them.

Kate sat thinking in an aimless way of all that had happened to her, and wishing that she could find something cheering in the prospect before her. Eventually her thoughts came back, as they often did, to Hervé, and she asked suddenly: 'Tell me, you said that Hervé left St Malo for his own reasons, not because of me. Why was that? You told him you'd found something out.'

Tristan shifted his position, as if stiff from sitting so long, and said, sounding slightly bored: 'Oh, that – I found only that he was in the pay of – an enemy – to work against me – or that someone was – and he knew that I should find soon that it was he. That's all. It was enough to make him fear my return. He would not have risked so much to help you.'

Kate reflected that it was a pity Hervé had

possessed such strong reasons for flight. If he had not, Tristan would have returned to St Malo to find her waiting for him still, and then perhaps he would not have been so angry with her. They could have travelled together to St Germain in the happy companionship which seemed now so far away. But perhaps she had caught him in an unusual good humour at St Malo; or perhaps he had merely been grateful for her entertaining qualities, and now that he no longer had need of them had no time for her either. After all, she had not known him for long before his illness, and then certainly not well enough to judge what he was really like. Perhaps this grimly silent man was the real Tristan de Plouvinel. It was a depressing thought.

It began to rain about mid-morning, which did not make the journey any more cheerful. Tristan talked little, and then only when absolutely necessary, and Kate was too low-spirited herself to try and coax him into a lighter mood. When they halted for dinner she had no appetite, and sat at their table in the inn parlour gazing gloomily at her plate. Tristan, already irritable, lost his temper at last, and shouted at her, whereupon she shouted in return, and then ran back to the coach in a sudden flood of tears. Tristan followed her, slamming the door of the coach behind him, and waving a lace-trimmed handkerchief in her face.

'It is considered ill-bred to lend one's handkerchief, but I think you have need of this. I did not think,' he added with disapproval, 'that you were the sort of woman who weeps.'

Kate took the handkerchief and blew her nose, glowering at him as she did so.

'You think I should endure everything in a meek silence do you?' she snapped tearfully. 'Just so long as I don't offend or embarrass you by showing what I really feel.'

Tristan raised his hands helplessly.

'What did I say? Nothing as I can remember. I was troubled only that you did not eat.'

'Then you have a very odd way of showing your concern!' she retorted. 'Why don't you leave me alone?'

'So I shall, with the greatest of pleasure,' he said. He called to the coachman to drive on and relapsed into a frowning silence which lasted until they reached the inn where they were to spend this first night of their journey. Kate was relieved to find herself alone at last in her room, and then wept again to think that she should feel so, when she had hoped for so much from this journey.

'He's right,' she thought angrily as she climbed into bed. 'I'm not the weeping kind of woman. But I'm turning into one, and that's no good at all.'

The inn was appalling. It was cold, and damp, and flea-ridden, and the service was surly in the extreme. Even Tristan's furious demands for better attention achieved no improvement, and since there was nowhere else to go they had to make the best of it. Kate came down in the morning in as gloomy a mood as that in which she had gone to bed, to find Tristan treating the inn-keeper to the most furiously blazing display of temper she had ever seen. The man looked cowed – as well he might – and Kate kept quietly out of the way until Tristan poured out a final stream of invective, flung a tiny fistful of coins on the dirty floor, and strode towards the waiting coach. She gathered, hurrying after him, that he had paid only half the bill, having told the innkeeper in eloquent and colourful terms exactly why he was doing so.

To her amazement, he smiled at her cheerfully as she took her seat.

'There – my feelings are relieved – I am

171

better. Now we shall find good food upon which to breakfast as we go, and we shall put that most infernal of places out of our minds. You are agreeable?'

Kate, smiling too, was entirely agreeable. In spite of everything the day was after all beginning well.

It continued to go well. The sun shone, and they ate at the roadside, stretched on the grass beneath the trees, at ease and laughing. Even last night's discomforts only provided something more to laugh about, a shared misfortune. It was a day when time seemed to stand still, when yesterday and tomorrow, and all their problems and complications, were as remote as the Pharaohs of Egypt, and as unimportant now to their present selves. Kate did not once worry about what lay at the end of the journey. She did not even think of her own coming unhappiness. She simply did as she had promised herself she would, and drained the last dregs of delight from the hours they passed together, happy simply to be in Tristan's company, feeling his hand brush hers as he passed bread for her to eat, watching the boyishly mischievous smile which turned her bones to water, aware always of his nearness, and thankful for every sweet moment of it.

The inn that night could not have contrasted more with last night's disastrous
lodging, and Kate woke refreshed next
morning ready to face the day with cheerfulness. Today they left Brittany behind them,
making a halt at Rennes where a newer and
more comfortable coach awaited them, sent
from Tristan's stables near St Malo: he had
sent word ahead for it to be ready. The
holiday mood of yesterday had gone. It was
only too easy, Kate found, to remember that
the end of their journey was almost in sight.
She was relieved though that the grimness
which had marred the early part of their
travels had not returned. Tristan's manner
was today brisk and business like, but at least
it did not shut her out.

'Tonight,' he explained as the new coach
carried them with speed along the improved
road, 'we stay at the house of a cousin of my
family. Only the Vicomtesse, his elderly
mother, will be there. He is at court, as
usual – he has no time for the country. But
we are expected.' He did not seem inclined
to talk any more, so Kate accepted the information in silence and gave her attention to
the passing countryside.

She had been dismayed by the neglected
state of Tristan's estates, but only too often

since she had been forced to concede that they looked positively well cared-for beside many of the villages through which they travelled. It was becoming commonplace to see tumbledown cottages, underfed cattle, weed-grown crops and thin hungry-looking children. Yet France, she had been led to believe, was a fertile land rich in natural resources. Something must be badly wrong for there to be such a general air of poverty everywhere. She was sure that a similar journey in England would only underline the contrast. She remembered very well the prosperous countryside around her aunt's home in Hampshire.

Towards evening, it grew worse. They were crossing lands so neglected that the stench of damp and dirt and decay reached them even behind the closed windows of the coach. The inhabitants, watching them pass, had a starved and sullen look which set Kate shivering. If they were close to tonight's resting place, then she was not sure that she wanted to arrive there. It could hardly offer them much in the way of comfort in the heart of this bleak landscape.

When the coach came to a halt Kate had fallen briefly asleep. She woke with a jerk as the footman opened the door and Tristan, jumping out, reached up to hand her down. And then, once in the open air, she stood quite still in amazement.

There, towering over the surrounding woods and the elaborate formal gardens, stood a château whose size and splendour took her breath away. It was like some palace in a fairy tale, a vast classical façade with wings running symmetrically at angles to the main building. It was new, and shining, and stunning in its magnificence. For the first time since she left St Malo Kate was acutely conscious of her thoroughly dishevelled appearance.

An army of liveried servants bowed them into a hall shining with polished wood and gilt and crystal. And there, waiting to greet them, stood the severe proud figure of Tristan's elderly distant cousin, the Vicomtesse, stiff in the elaborate splendour of full court dress. She greeted them with a chilly formality which only increased Kate's sense of inferiority.

'So this,' she concluded, cold eyes running over Kate in a kind of icy disbelief, 'is the young girl who is to go to St Germain? I see the problem.'

'What problem?' thought Kate, reddening. She glanced at Tristan, but his face was an impassive mask, all cool courtesy to match that of his kinswoman.

'You may safely leave her in my hands,' the Vicomtesse went on, and before she knew what was happening Kate found herself being steered towards a wide staircase. A succession of passages, and wide painted rooms, and yet more stairs brought the two women at last to a small attic room where a weary-looking sewing girl sat at work. Two other servants appeared, and the Vicomtesse issued a barrage of instructions with such speed that Kate could not take them in. The next moment efficient hands were stripping her to her shift and pulling over her head the heavy silken folds of a silver-grey gown, low-necked, long-waisted, ruffled and ribbon-trimmed. It must have been made for someone else, for it was far too big, and the Vicomtesse stood observing Kate with that dauntingly critical eye as the servants pinned and tucked at her command. Kate wondered if the old lady thought of her as a human being at all. 'I see the problem,' she had said, as if Kate were simply a poorly-clad doll.

The problem, clearly, must have been Kate's appearance. And Kate realised now with a sudden rising burst of fury, that

Tristan must have notified his cousin of this 'problem' when he told her they were on their way, perhaps even then enlisting her aid. The speed with which Kate had been taken in hand suggested that she had been forewarned. That, then, told Kate only too clearly what Tristan thought of her: a problem, to be solved when she was delivered safely at St Germain dressed, presumably, in something other than the travel-worn clothes she had been wearing on the *Proud Lady*. It was not the first time he had shown concern about what she wore. Perhaps he felt it damaged his reputation if his companion did not match him in finery. If he had been in the room with her now, Kate would have told him exactly what she thought of his behaviour, in words sharpened by her own hurt at being spoken of so casually and dismissively.

But he was not here, and before long the Vicomtesse had gone too. The gown was removed, so that the seamstress could begin work on altering it, and Kate was led to another room where perfumed water was ready for her to wash herself – or rather, for the servants to wash her, a process which irritated and embarrassed her. By the time they had finished, the gown too was ready, and they dressed her in it with an almost reverential care. Then they bound up her hair into the closest approximation possible to a fashionable coiffure, and fastened upon it a high lace fontage, the stiffly elaborate headdress worn by all well-dressed ladies, its lacy veil falling to her shoulders. There were silk stockings and high-heeled silver slippers for her feet, and even a necklace of pearls about her throat. And then she was ready, only too certain that she must look ridiculous as she made her way, tight-laced, poised and rustling, after the servant down the stairs to where Tristan and the Vicomtesse waited in the parlour for her to join them for supper.

They looked up as she came in, and the thin lips of the Vicomtesse moved in what was most probably the closest she ever came to a smile. A gleam of approval lit her eyes. 'That is better,' she commented.

Kate glanced at Tristan, her eyes bright with an anger which she hoped he would interpret correctly. If only they had been alone she would have done more than glare. But he seemed unaware of her anger. He was looking at her with an expression of unmistakable amazement. 'If he laughs,' thought Kate fiercely, 'I shall never forgive him!' This was one time when laughter would be most definitely unacceptable.

But he did not laugh. In fact he frowned, as if some new and disturbing thought had occurred to him; and then he turned to thank the Vicomtesse with elaborate courtesy for the trouble she had taken.

Supper was a slow and impressive meal, its rigid formality matched by the conversation which took place over it. That effectively shut Kate out from any part in it, for she could not hope to rival the Vicomtesse and Tristan in the solemn triviality of their talk. It was a revelation to her that Tristan could be so monumentally boring. But then perhaps the Vicomtesse found the conversation to her taste.

Kate's bedroom, when at last, with relief, she was led to it, was the grandest she had ever experienced. The bed, of course, was as yieldingly soft as its curtains were rich and glowing. But she did not sleep well. She wondered in fact if anyone could sleep well in such a place, where every piece of furniture, every gilded decoration, every embroidered garment seemed designed to declare to the world how wealthy and prestigious its owner was. She remembered, uncomfortably, the hovels they had passed today, and wondered that the owner of this place could ever feel at home in this contrasting luxury. Perhaps that was why he preferred to remain at court.

A long breakfast, as tedious as last night's supper, had to be endured before Tristan's coach was brought to the door and he and Kate could take their leave of the Vicomtesse. Now at last, thought Kate, as they moved away from the château, they were alone, and she could bring up the matter foremost in her mind.

'I do not like being referred to as a problem. I am not a problem. And I do not wish to be dressed up like some mindless doll.'

Tristan turned to look at her in surprise, and then a mild amusement lit his face.

'You do not look in the least like a doll,' he reassured her. 'And that you have a mind I know very well. What troubles you? You surely cannot have wished to arrive at St Germain as you were?'

'Why not? I wasn't ashamed of my appearance. You can't expect to spend several weeks in the hands of a pirate and come out of it looking fresh as a daisy.'

Tristan frowned at her final sentence, and said stiffly: 'The King of England may be an exile, but St Germain is still his court, and to arrive there in a state of unnecessary disarray would be grave discourtesy.'

'You sound just like the Vicomtesse,' retorted Kate. 'I can well believe you are related.'

He seemed about to give an angry answer, but thought better of it and said: 'Do not let us quarrel. I meant it only in kindness. I think you will be grateful.'

Kate pursed her lips and looked out of the window. They had left behind the beautiful gardens and the forest, and had emerged into an undulating landscape scattered with villages as poor as those they had passed yesterday.

'Does all this belong to your cousin at the château?' asked Kate.

'Yes,' said Tristan. 'He is one of the wealthiest man in France, and his estates are extensive.' Kate gave a little cry of indignation.

'I think it's a disgrace.'

'What is? What is wrong?'

Kate indicated the scene beyond the window.

'All that wealth – the château and the food and the clothes and the furniture, and the army of servants, all for one old woman–'

'My cousin comes sometimes, for the hunting.'

'And rides over the farmers' crops, I suppose?'

Tristan smiled faintly. 'Very likely,' he conceded, in an amused tone which merely roused her indignation still further.

'It's not funny! Not in the least bit funny! How can you even think it, when those people out there live in the most terrible poverty? They're his tenants, I suppose, and he has all that wealth – why does he not improve the land and mend the houses and employ a doctor and set up schools, and take care of his people? Why is he wasting his time at court when there's so much to be done here?'

'Because,' replied Tristan carefully, 'the King requires that his nobility live in a style to accord with their rank, and he demands their presence at court.'

'I'm sure the King would rather they looked after their estates.'

'I think you are mistaken. You see, Miss Kate, the King sees himself as a most glorious sun, the centre of the universe. He wishes always to be surrounded by his constellations, the lesser reflections of his glory. What happens in the outer darkness where his rays do not reach does not concern him.

'I think,' declared Kate stoutly, 'it would be a much finer reflection of his glory if his people lived in prosperity – all his people, that is, not just his nobility. Don't you agree?'

Tristan smiled and shook his head.

'Ah, Miss Kate, it is always the same! As with my garden – you would set it to rights at once.'

'Of course,' said Kate. 'Or at least I should make the attempt.'

Tristan was silent for a moment, watching her with a thoughtful expression. Then he said gently: 'A clear head and a warm heart – it is a good combination you have, English Miss Kate.'

She felt her colour rise under his approval, and tried hard to think of something suitable to say. But he spared her the necessity by saying next, in quite a different tone: 'Miss Kate, you are outspoken, and that I like, that you should be always so honest. But not all will listen and keep quiet, as I do–'

'Quiet!' she burst in, wide eyed and laughing. He smiled. 'I mean to say,' he explained patiently, 'that I do not repeat what you say to others, who would look on it less kindly. Be careful – in every court, there are ears where you least expect them – and King Louis has his friends every-where. He is a great and generous King –

but his tolerance has its limits.'

Kate stared at him, slowly taking in the implications, and then she shivered. Perhaps he read the dismay in her face, for he said reassuringly: 'You need not be afraid – only careful. As I am.'

The thought of Tristan being careful was so ludicrous that Kate laughed; but she remembered his conversation last night at supper, and thought perhaps he was right after all. When the need arose, he could be discretion itself. She was reminded that he was not simply a blunt captain of corsairs, but also a nobleman and a courtier, with years of experience of the world and its ways behind him. She felt all at once very young and green and ignorant.

They came to St Germain at dusk, the coach-horses struggling up the steep hill to the old château in which King James's court was housed. Kate knew without being told that they had arrived: misery settled like a dead weight over her heart. She was surprised that Tristan seemed as gloomily withdrawn as she: he had said nothing for a long time now.

The coach swung between two vast gateposts and came to a halt. Servants came running, torches held high, flames streaming behind them, and the coach door was flung wide. Hands reached up to assist Kate to descend, for all the world as if she were indeed the grand lady she appeared, stepping on to the gravel in second-hand silver slippers, one small slim hand holding her silver skirts free of the dust, the light wind lifting the lace of her little veil, and ruffling the fur of the sable tippet which the Vicomtesse had wrapped about her shoulders at their parting. Not far away lanterns and torches lit a great stone doorway, surmounted by intricate carving; and from its bright opening emerged a stout, bewigged figure who came towards her, smiling, with outstretched arms; and who she realised only just in time was her brother Harry.

Laughing suddenly, she ran into his arms, all her dignity gone in a moment.

'Oh, Harry, dear Harry! You've grown so plump I didn't know you!'

He exclaimed in mock indignation at her greeting, but his welcome was as warm as she could have wished. The smell of tobacco and wine which hung about him was, lamentably, just as she remembered it. She was all at once swept back eight years to the happy child she had been when Harry went away. He had not really changed: dear wild Harry, her beloved scapegrace of a brother.

But there was someone dearer still who must not go before she had said goodbye. She released herself from Harry's embrace and looked round just in time to see Tristan climbing back into the coach. She ran, calling: 'Wait – don't go!'

He turned, pausing on the step of the coach, looking down at her questioningly. His expression was grave, severe almost, and his face pale. She thought perhaps he disapproved of her undignified behaviour; but he had never minded before.

'I … I wanted to say goodbye properly,' she said hesitantly. 'And to thank you.'

He stepped down to stand facing her. His nearness was unbearable here in this public place, before all those watching eyes, where she could not touch him, or say to him anything which was not fit for everyone else to hear. It seemed as if her whole self ached to feel his arms about her, his mouth on hers. Instead, she stood smiling stiffly, and tried to speak through a desperately con-stricted throat.

'You have been kind,' she said, thinking how very inadequate that sounded. He indi-cated his head with all the distant courtesy

186

he had shown to the Vicomtesse.

'You also,' he returned, his voice tight and clipped. She felt almost as if she were trying to make conversation with a stranger. It hurt her terribly to be parting from him like this, and the tears rushed to her eyes. But he must not see them, and she sniffed and broadened that unconvincing smile while she tried to think of something else to say. Only her mind was empty of all but the need to find the right words to take her leave as she should. In the end, it was he who spoke next, and she knew sickeningly that this was irrevocably the final leave-taking.

'I wish you well, Miss Kate: you and Mr William Harwood. I offer you my most sincere good wishes for your future happiness.'

Kate shivered in the cold little wind that seemed suddenly to have arisen, and opened her mouth to speak, but no words came. And the next moment he had taken her hand in his and bent his head and pressed it to his lips. Then murmuring some parting words she did not quite hear he turned away and leapt into the coach, slamming the door, and the coachman urged the horses forward. Kate stood quite still, staring as the coach rumbled away. He had kissed her hand once before, but not like this, not with this burning intensity which seemed to sear her flesh, so that she almost expected to find the scorch mark clearly imprinted on her skin. Or was it just her imagination, born of the intense emotions which hurt her so, the horrible burning pain of separation that left her feeling as if she had been torn apart? It was as if half of herself had gone in that departing coach.

Slowly, what was left of Kate Pendleton turned and made its way back to where her brother was waiting.

Eleven

The old château of St Germain, out of date and inconvenient, had inadequate room for all the exiles and hangers on and their various families and households who surrounded King James. But Harry Pendleton had a minor and undemanding post at court, and as a consequence a small suite of rooms on the second floor had been placed at his disposal. And so there, in relative comfort, he was able to accommodate his sister.

On that first evening he showed her with marked pride into the cramped room where she would sleep, and then the more spacious apartment where a light supper was waiting. Tristan had sent someone ahead to herald her arrival, so that she should be sure of a welcome.

'Afraid it's not much,' said Harry in an apologetic tone which lacked conviction. 'But it'll do you I'm sure. You'll not be here long – I'll see you get on your way to Ireland as soon as possible.'

Kate felt her stomach give a sickening

lurch. In Brittany her marriage had seemed very remote, something she must face eventually, but not yet; not, at the very least, until she had savoured some of the excitements of St Germain. And now Harry was speaking of it as an event to be worked for with all speed.

'I can't marry William!' The panic-stricken words rang soundlessly in her head, an instinctive reaction to Harry's plan. But she could not say them aloud. She wanted very much to explain something of what she felt to Harry. She had tender memories of his constant sympathetic understanding. But that had been a very long time ago, and however much she might feel at home with him now she knew they could not return at once to that old easy relationship, if for no other reason than that she was a woman now, and not the child he remembered. Perhaps that would mean they could be closer than ever, but she could not yet be sure. And she was very tired, and far too miserable to think clearly, and she knew she must have some time alone to face up to her own feelings.

She was glad that the meal provided an excuse not to talk, though in fact she ate very little. Harry, she noticed, felt no such lack of appetite, and he drank even more deeply than he ate. She lost count of the number of times he refilled his glass, though he did not show any sign that the drink had adversely affected him in any way.

When Harry realised at last that Kate was no longer making any attempt to eat, he said: 'You'll be tired, Kate. Get yourself to bed. We'll talk about what's to be done in the morning.' And she was only too thankful to act on his suggestion at once.

'What's to be done': the phrase lingered in her thoughts as she closed the door of her room behind her and began slowly to undress. If Harry was to discuss the matter with her in the morning, then she must know what she herself wanted to do. Yet in her present frame of mind she could not trust her own judgement. She knew very well that if anyone had turned to her now, weighed down as she was with the memory of that painful parting from Tristan de Plouvinel, she would have said without hesitation: 'I *cannot* marry William Harwood.'

But she was betrothed, and if it had not been for Tristan de Plouvinel she would have been Mrs Harwood by now. She must not allow this evening's deep emotions to affect her whole life. If her spirit rebelled against her eminently suitable marriage, that was only to be expected in her present mood. She must rest now, and then in the morning her head would be clearer, more ready to make the vital decisions that faced her. After all, Harry would very likely be happy for her to stay with him for longer than he had clearly expected, if she were to make him understand how much she wanted it. She climbed slowly into the narrow bed, and pulled the blankets over her and closed her eyes.

She slept for much of the night, but there were long intervals during which she lay awake staring into the darkness, tormented by thoughts and memories which seemed to go round and round in circles, never coming to any conclusion. She fell asleep for a last time as dawn broke, and it seemed only a moment afterwards that the steady noisy clamour of a bell ringing from somewhere outside woke her again. She listened for a moment, irritated at being disturbed, and then turned over to sleep again. As she did so the full recollection of last night's parting hit her like a blow, reviving her misery in all its aching freshness. She wondered dully how long it would be before she could think of Tristan de Plouvinel without pain.

In the end, she realised that it was useless trying to sleep again, and got up and dressed. She went first to the window. It led on to a long balcony which ran around the whole second floor of the building, and looked out over a courtyard enclosed on its five irregular sides by the high walls of the château, its severity relieved only by a tiny formal garden, an austere arrangement of low clipped hedges and trim grass.

The bell had ceased ringing, but its cause was evident. At one side of the courtyard rose the elaborate gothic tracery of a chapel, and towards it now two men and a woman were hurrying with the unmistakable air of worshippers late for a service. Otherwise the courtyard was empty, but for a gardener weeding the narrow stretch of earth at the base of the hedges. He must have been cold, Kate thought, for though the sky far overhead was clear and blue and cloudless, and the balustraded roof gilded with sunlight, the yard was still in deep shadow, the grass heavily dewed.

Kate left the window and went into the room where they had eaten last night. The air was thick with tobacco smoke, stale and choking, and several empty bottles and a well-used glass indicated how Harry had spent the evening. There was no sign of her brother, however. She pushed open a further door and looked inside.

A dishevelled bed met her eyes, piled high with disordered bedclothes. A shaven brown head was just visible, its owner motionless and snoring. Wig and clothes lay scattered about the floor. Harry, Kate guessed with affectionate exasperation, had gone late and very drunk, to bed last night. He would certainly not be stirring for some considerable time.

She had time then to face the question which had haunted her so fruitlessly through the wakeful hours of the night. Softly, she closed Harry's door, and opened a window to clear the air of the stuffy living room, and then stood gazing out, all her thoughts concentrated on the problem of her future.

Only now, all at once, it was no longer a problem. She knew exactly what she was going to do, and what she was not going to do. She knew, first of all, that somehow she must learn to put Tristan de Plouvinel behind her, as he had most certainly done with her. If she could not forget him, then she must at least learn to think of him without pain. And to do that her life must be filled with new interests and activities, and new friendships. If she were to marry William she would be going to a man, and a way of life, totally different from anything she might ever have known with Tristan. But it would be a life that would offer her nothing to help her forget, only long tedious unfilled hours when she would have only her memories to amuse her. Further, everything about William would only remind her by contrast how wonderful and exciting a companion Tristan de Plouvinel had been. No, if she were ever to be married it must be to a man who could make her forget, and that William could not begin to do. If she went to Ireland, she would put hundreds of miles between herself and the man she loved, but she would be prolonging that love, and its inevitable heartache, for as long as she lived. If nothing else, she thought, that would be unfair to William.

Her mind was made up. She would stay here with Harry, and allow the distractions of the court to fill her days, and new friendships to console her for her loss. It was the only possible choice she could make, in the circumstances.

It was nearly midday when Harry at last got up, stumbling into the room half-dressed, yawning and rubbing his eyes. He had almost collided with Kate before he realised she was there. Last night had clearly become no more than a dim blur in his memory, and he peered at her for some time, as if trying to remember who she was. Then he found a bottle, and poured himself a drink, and stood looking at her thoughtfully.

'That may be all you have for breakfast,' said Kate with feeling, 'but I'm hungry, and it must be just about dinner time.'

Harry glanced at the ornate clock on the mantelpiece.

'Aye, so it is.' He stretched. 'You been up long? You should've shouted for something.' She was relieved when, after a moment's consideration, he softened and ordered food to be brought. She ate hungrily, already feeling greatly refreshed.

'Some people got up early,' she told him, with a faintly reproachful tone. 'I watched them go to the chapel.'

'You *were* up early!' commented her brother wonderingly. 'You could have gone too, if you'd wanted. But it doesn't matter – plenty more opportunities. They go to church all the time here. Very devout man, the King.'

Since King James's Catholicism had been the cause of his downfall, Kate did not find that very surprising, so she made no comment. She could not image Harry as a devoted churchgoer, however, so she asked: 'What do you do with yourself all the time?'

He shrugged.

'This and that – hunting, cards – we go to Versailles sometimes.' He poured himself a further glass of wine, and then looked at Kate. 'When are you to wed this Harwood fellow?'

'We should have been married in July,' said Kate. She paused, trying to find the right way to approach what was uppermost in her mind, and then asked: 'How did you know about him? I didn't think you had news from home.'

'Same as I knew where you were,' said Harry. 'From the Marquise de Tacoignières.'

The beautiful and ageless Marguerite, to whom Tristan owed all he had. Kate felt her heart twist with anguished jealousy. What kind of woman must she be, to earn the devotion of such a man?

'You know her then – what's she like?'

Harry shrugged again.

'Very astute woman. And very powerful. If she wants something, she gets it. It's said the King – King Louis, that is – it's said he bedded her once, before Madame de Maintenon came along. Still, I wouldn't know about that. They say she has the King's ear though.'

And Tristan's heart, added Kate to herself. She left the table and went to the window.

'Harry,' she began quickly, for fear that some impulse might make her change her mind after all, and that she would then regret it for ever. 'I'm not going to Ireland.'

Harry set down his glass, and stared at her.

'Why ever not? Mr Harwood coming here for you, is that it?'

Kate smiled faintly at the very idea.

'No,' she said. 'I'm not going to marry him. I shall write to him and tell him so.'

'Kate!– You can't do that!'

She turned to look at him, almost amused by the look of appalled dismay on his face.

'Why not?'

'Well – because you're betrothed, and you can't just change your mind. What would they all say of you? Besides, why should you want to? – He sounds a good match to me – money, land, all that kind of thing. Just what a girl needs in a husband.'

'But not what I need,' said Kate quietly, coming to sit down again. It mattered very much to her that she should be able to make

Harry understand. 'I just know I could never be happy with him – we're quite unsuited. He's good and kind, but very respectable and correct and dull – and I am not. You know that, don't you?'

'What does it matter? A woman in your position can't pick and choose. Just be thankful you've got such a good match. You can put up with the rest, can't you?'

'No – no, I can't. In any case, I'm not so very badly off. You know Grandfather left me a generous sum to provide a dowry?'

'No, I didn't.' He gave the matter some consideration, and then observed: 'If that's so you'll have to marry first, before you get anything.'

'Perhaps – but it also means I am free to choose how I marry.'

Enlightenment lit Harry's face.

'Ah, I see! There's someone else you want to wed! That's it, isn't it? Someone Aunt Tabby and the uncles don't hold with perhaps? And now you've got away you intend to do as you please?'

'If only it were true, and as easy as that,' thought Kate. She shook her head.

'No – no, I haven't a husband in mind. I just know I can't marry William.'

Harry raised his hands in exasperation.

'I don't understand you, Kate. I didn't think you were one of those silly women who changed their minds at every daft whim. But if you turn down this William, that's what you'll be.'

'Don't you mind that he's a supporter of King William, a Whig to the backbone.'

'Doesn't bother me. You're a woman – politics don't matter to you. You make a good marriage – that's all that matters.'

This morning, waiting for Harry to get up, Kate had imagined telling him all about Tristan, and how she loved him, and yet could hope for nothing from him; and how because of that love she could not marry William. But now all at once she knew she could not tell Harry any of it. She felt as if she were trying to find some familiar land-mark in a misty landscape, something to show her the way back to a place she knew, where she would be safe. But there were no landmarks. Harry, drinking steadily, seemed to be totally unable to understand what she was trying to say. Once, long ago, she had told him everything, and always been sure that he would care and would sympathise. But she realised now, with what was almost a steadily mounting panic, that this pre-maturely middle-aged man was no longer the brother she had loved, but someone quite different, who in the years of separation had grown totally apart from her. The realisation did not make her change her mind about William, but she ceased trying to tell Harry why she had made her choice.

'If I do make a good marriage, it won't be to William Harwood. I've decided – and that's it.'

Harry stared gloomily into his now empty glass, twisting it in his fingers.

'What will you do then?'

'I'd hoped,' said Kate, a little uncertainly, 'that I could stay here with you.' She wished she had not looked up in time to catch the expression of undisguised dismay on his face.

He was silent for some time, and then cleared his throat twice, with vigour, and said: 'Oh – well – yes. Very welcome, of course– But I can't help thinking you'd be better wed. Still, leave it a bit – think about it – give it time. You don't want to be hasty about things like that – could be just a passing fancy, you know, this wanting to break it off.'

'It's not – and I shall write today,' was Kate's reply. She told herself too that she would not allow herself to be depressed by

Harry's lack of enthusiasm for her company. He would grow used to the idea, perhaps even come to like it. And meanwhile she might think of some other solution to the vexed question of her future.

Later that day, still under protest from Harry, she borrowed pen and ink and sat down to write to William. She had not thought it would be easy, but she did not expect it to be quite so difficult to find the right words. She knew he did not love her, but in his own way he liked her very much, and that he would be hurt by her rejection was inevitable. What she did not want was that his pride also should be hurt by too public an ending of their betrothal. In the end, after several false beginnings and much chewing of her quill, she wrote that though she liked and respected him she had come to the firm conclusion that she could never be his wife. She was sure it was for the best, for his happiness as well as her own. She hoped he would soon find a wife much more suited to him in temperament and accomplishments. And she ended finally with the generous suggestion that he could blacken her name as much as he wished to his friends, if that would salve his pride. He might, for instance, she suggested, let it be known that she had been seduced and corrupted by her pirate captors: or that she had turned passionately Jacobite and thrown in her lot completely with the exiled King. It did not matter what he said, for Ireland was a long way off and she was never, now, likely to come there. It was possible that she would not now even return to England, or not for a very long time.

She wept a little over the letter, because it would hurt William, however careful she had been, and perhaps too because it marked the end of an era in her life, and ushered in an unknown and rather frightening future. 'What,' she thought with a kind of terror, 'if all the excitement is over, and all the happiness I shall ever know, and all the love – and I have only emptiness left?' But she told herself very severely not to be fanciful, and sealed the letter with Harry's seal, and asked him to see that it was sent safely on its way as soon as possible. Harry complained again at her rashness, but he promised to do as she wished.

She went to bed that night with her spirits lightened by a sense of relief. One unpleasant duty at least had been done. She was free at last.

Only it was not freedom but aimlessness

which seemed to mark her days now. She felt like a leaf caught in the wind, blown hither and thither without purpose; or like that tiny boat tossed on the angry waves on that dreadful night she still could not think of without a shudder of horror. In fact, the whole exiled court seemed to be afflicted with the same sense of futility. With a treaty between France and England under negotiation, hopes of an early restoration of King James to his lost throne were receding fast. The most ardent loyalists continued to plot; but King James turned more than ever to the consolations of his religion; and the barely religious, like Harry, filled the time as best they could with largely meaningless activities.

Harry's main consolation, as Kate realised after only a day or two at St Germain, was drink. He had always drunk deep, rolling home in the small hours after some convivial gathering, and waking late in the day with an aching head. But now there were few convivial gatherings, and the drinking began when he crawled out of bed – even before, for all Kate knew – and went on all day, with a kind of remorseless steadiness. That he rarely appeared drunk was no reassurance at all, for it only showed how very accustomed he was to drinking. And it had affected him in subtler ways. As he had grown stout in body, so he had grown slow and stolid in mind. His old energy, his sense of fun, his delight in new things, his quick wit had all gone, and left no trace behind. Drink had destroyed the old Harry, and in his place now was a bored, unhappy, disillusioned man. Kate, having tried once or twice without success to remonstrate with him, resigned herself to learning to live with this new and unappealing brother, her despair at his state softened only by a desperate pity.

It was easy enough, too, she thought ruefully, to see what had made him take to drink. Dependent largely on the charity of the French court, King James's courtiers had little money to spend on entertainments or luxuries. The court's social life was limited in the extreme, as much as anything else by the King's pious rejection of frivolity. The occasional excursion to Versailles brought the only break in deadly routine. 'So much,' thought Kate bleakly, 'for a ceaseless round of new activities to help me forget Tristan de Plouvinel!'

Even the distractions of friendship seemed to be denied to her. The court seemed to consist of the young and disillusioned, like Harry, or the old and pious, like the King himself. There were no kindred spirits, eager and full of enthusiasm and love of life, with whom she could walk in the beautiful gardens laid out on the hillside between the château and the forest beyond; no companions with whom to ride deep into the enchantingly lovely forest, sharing talk and laughter and warm friendship. She felt more alone than she had ever been in her life before, except perhaps during that terrible time imprisoned in Hervé's house. 'If it goes on like this,' she thought one day, 'I shall go out of my mind for good.' She even began to think in her more despairing moments that Harry had been right, and she had been too hasty in breaking off her marriage to William. Surely marriage to him could never have been so stupifyingly, destructively tedious as this? But then she remembered that marriage was permanent, and life at St Germain was not, or only if she chose to make it so. In time, surely, she must find some satisfactory alternative to depending on Harry's reluctant hospitality.

A temporary solution did offer itself. King James's Queen, Mary of Modena, suddenly and unexpectedly took a hand in the affair of the newest arrival at her court, and offered to Kate the honour of becoming one of her ladies in waiting. Kate, astonished, and aware that she ought to show real gratitude, stammered out clumsily that she did not know if she should accept; that she might not wish to stay at St Germain. Queen Mary, quite untroubled, suggested that such a post might give her a strong position from which to consider her future. She would have companions, the certainty for as long as she wished of a roof over her head and clothes to wear, and something to occupy her time. And she would no longer be dependent on Harry. One look at her brother's delighted expression when she told him of the offer convinced Kate, and she accepted.

She had no cause to regret the decision. Her duties were light and not very interesting, and her fellow ladies in waiting were for the most part devout and serious-minded and not very enlivening company, but the Queen was a gentle and kindly woman, and Kate grew fond of her, and grateful for the care she showed for all those about her. She began to feel just a little more optimistic about her future.

Then one bright day in October, when the forest was glowing with bronze and apricot, gold and copper and fiery red, King Louis and half his court came from Versailles to hunt. Now at last the air was electric with excitement, the château buzzing with preparations – food fit for so splendid a King, to be carried into the forest to refresh the huntsmen, riding coats to be freshly embroidered, hats newly plumed, horses groomed until they shone like polished armour. Even Harry drank a little less that day; and there was almost the old sparkle in his eyes. Kate wore a borrowed coat of dark red velvet richly laid with silver: it was a little too large for her, but looked well over the grey silk, with a plumed hat (also borrowed) to complete the costume. Beside the elaborate riding costumes of the ladies from Versailles it was only too evident that the clothes were not her own, but she was too happy at this brief respite to her boredom to mind very much.

She had one fear only, though she was not quite sure if it was a fear or a hope: that Tristan would be there. She did not know if she could bear to see him again before she had learned to accept that he was a part of her past, gone and lost to her for ever. But she told herself that he did not come often to court, and he had said he was eager to go to sea again, and very likely her fears were unfounded.

Even so, her eyes scanned the crowd anxiously as she rode out with the little group from St Germain to join the French King's party, fearfully seeking that dark head towering over the lesser mortals about him. But she saw no one even to remind her of him, and relief swept her, mingled with the faintest trace of disappointment. It was just as well. Now she could relax and enjoy herself.

In the end, however, the occasion proved an anticlimax. The ride in the forest, on a passable horse, trotting through dappled sunlight in the crisp bright air, the glades misted with gold, was pure delight. But the company was not. Haughty ladies and supercilious noblemen gazed down their noses at Kate in marked disdain. Even their riding costumes, she noted, had more gold embroidery than any of her clothes had ever possessed. And perhaps, too, these painted and patched and perfumed courtiers found her rosy freckled complexion unbecomingly unadorned. She would not have minded any of it if she could have had a congenial companion to ride at her side; but Harry very soon disappeared in search of refreshment, and few of Queen Mary's ladies cared to ride. In any case, she thought ruefully, if there had been anyone to ride with her they would very likely soon have flocked with all the others to join the fawning crowd about King Louis, hoping for an approving look, or better still the sought-after crumbs of a few treasured words from his royal lips to fall upon them. The hunt itself was clearly very much of secondary importance. She wondered if even the King enjoyed it.

When they halted in a wide glade to eat, Kate sat on the grass near the two or three of Queen Mary's ladies who had ventured out, and studied the crowd. The King was eating now – a gilded chair and table had been brought for him – and the flatterers hovered round him still like flies, getting in the way of the servants, foregoing their own meal for the greater satisfaction of serving their King. Disgusted, Kate looked away to where the less importunate courtiers had settled themselves to eat in groups, and at the far side of the glade where a number of coaches had been driven along a straight road through the forest to bring the less energetic or healthy to join the merriment. Liveried servants carried food and drink to them as they sat sheltered from the air in their luxurious silk and velvet-lined vehicles.

Eventually the feasting was done, the

servants scurried to clear away the debris, and the word went out that the hunt was resumed. Kate mounted, wondering whether to go off by herself for a solitary ride. It would be delightful on this lovely day, much pleasanter than to linger in the stifling atmosphere of this royal hunt. But Harry had warned her that it was only too easy to lose oneself in the forest, so she repressed her impulse and turned to follow the court.

At that moment Harry himself suddenly appeared and caught at her rein. She could see by his face that he had made up for lost time with his drinking.

'I didn't know you were here,' she said. 'I didn't see you.'

'Oh, I was around–' he said vaguely. Then he went on: 'The Marquise de Tacoignières wants a word with you.'

Her heart gave a painful twist. Marguerite – Tristan's Marguerite – wanted to see her. She glanced round quickly, wondering which of the arrogant, beautiful ladies she had seen today was that most fortunate of women. But most of the riders had gone; and Harry waved towards the coaches.

'Over there – I'll show you,' and he led her towards one of the ornate and gilded vehicles. He left her to ride the last few yards alone. She wondered whether to dismount and decided against it. At least on horseback her head was level with the coach window. On foot she would be at a disadvantage.

A face appeared at the window, a face so grotesque that for an instant she drew rein, stilled by shock. It was like a mask, enamelled in white and overlaid with vivid pink, adorned with a silken patch night-dark on the too-smooth cheekbone, the unnaturally bright-gold hair intricately curled about that puppet face beneath the most elaborate fontage Kate had ever seen. A white hand, thin and claw-like, clutched the rim of the open window, its nails red-tinted.

'Come here, girl,' commanded a voice of imperious iciness, which reminded Kate for a moment of the Vicomtesse. Reluctantly, unable to take her eyes from the spectacle before her, like some hideous doll, she drew nearer. This must be some dragon guardian of Marguerite's, she supposed, keeping unwelcome admirers from troubling her beautiful mistress. Kate acknowledged that she was likely to be only too successful.

Yet when she reached the coach she could see no one else inside, and she hesitated, a little unsure of herself. Had Harry directed her to the wrong coach? In his drunken state it was only too likely.

'I was told,' she explained in her clear sweet tones, their warmth contrasting markedly with the haughtiness of the other woman's voice, 'that the Marquise de Tacoignières wished to speak to me.'

'Of course,' said the puppet, a little impatiently, 'that is why you are here. I required your brother to send you. I was anxious to see what manner of young girl Monsieur le Comte de Plouvinel had brought back as his booty.' She said 'young girl' as if the words implied all kinds of unmentionable immoralities. Kate was just wondering exactly what she meant by it when a horrible, sickening realisation struck her with all the force of a blow. This – this dreadful painted harridan, in whom no traces of the real person beneath were left, but only the false and painstakingly fashioned surface – this grotesque caricature of youth believable as such only from a great distance – *this* was Marguerite de Tacoignières, ageless, beautiful for whom that lovely and deadly ship had been named, as a tribute from the man who had given her his heart.

How was it possible?

It was not possible! Shivering with repugnance, Kate stared at the woman before her and tried to grasp the truth, and to understand it. He could not love her, surely, not Tristan de Plouvinel who had played cards with Kate Pendleton, and laughed and teased, and raged at his servants, and held her in his arms? How could that emotional, quick-tempered, impulsive man whom she thought she knew have anything to do with this hideous shell of a woman before her? Marguerite had, years before, paid for him to go to sea. Perhaps then she had been young and beautiful indeed, and only with the years gone to these terrible lengths to try and preserve something of what she once had possessed. Perhaps gratitude kept Tristan faithful when all passion must have gone. Or did she, Kate Pendleton, know nothing of the real Tristan de Plouvinel, and was he able, coldly and with careful calculation, to offer something like devotion and passion to this woman? Could he even love her, with the blindness that poets spoke of?

'What are you staring at, girl?' The sharp voice broke into her thoughts, and she blushed uncomfortably. 'And have you no manners, to remain mounted before your betters.'

Kate would have liked to make some angry

retort; but she was an impoverished guest in a foreign land, and this woman was said to have the ear of the most powerful monarch in Europe, and so, fuming inwardly, she slid to the ground. Marguerite's eyes ran over her, noting without mercy the cast off clothes, the too slim figure, the protruding teeth, and all the other deficiencies of which Kate was only too aware. 'So much for my disapproval of her appearance,' thought Kate ruefully. 'Perhaps she knows what I was thinking.'

'So,' said Marguerite at last, with a note of satisfaction in her voice, 'I can see why he parted so readily with his prize – I do not imagine he can have hoped for much of a ransom. You are no radiant beauty, are you, girl? But I understand that you have turned down an excellent husband. That was singularly foolish of you. What do you hope to gain by it? One needs more than you have to shine at court, you know.'

'I don't want to shine at court, thank you!' retorted Kate with asperity, only just preventing herself from adding: 'And certainly not if you're an example of what one must become!'

'That is just as well,' said Marguerite. 'What are your plans then? It seems to me you have shockingly mishandled your own affairs.'

'But at least it is my doing and no one else's,' Kate returned, hoping that the implied message: 'Mind your own business!' would reach her inquisitor. If it did, Marguerite showed no sign of it.

'I hope it gives you satisfaction to be the agent of your own downfall,' she observed. 'For you are certainly heading fast for disaster. Foolish girl!' She paused, her pale disdainful eyes running once more over the erect and now inwardly fuming figure before her. 'Tristan de Plouvinel is at sea again, as I expect you will have guessed.'

The sudden change of subject took Kate by surprise.

'Oh, is he?' she replied, trying to sound nonchalant about it.

'It is likely that this will be his last voyage, or almost his last. The King is seeking peace with his enemies. There will no longer be a need for corsairs to preserve the safety of this kingdom. I think too that Tristan de Plouvinel is inclined to seek a less adventurous career – at court, perhaps, where he will certainly be welcome. And of course a rich marriage is essential. He has made a great deal, of course, but life at court is ruinously expensive. A financier's daughter should suit him, I think – no birth or breeding, of course, but a fortune compensates for that. And one can still seek one's pleasures elsewhere–'

'Why is she telling me all this?' thought Kate, through the painful disorder of her feelings. 'It is almost as if she wants to hurt me or to warn me off. Can she know what I feel – or does she think I broke off my marriage to William because I hoped to win Tristan?' But that last was a ridiculous idea, and if Marguerite thought it, Kate wondered how she could have come to do so. Harry must have told her of the end of the betrothal, but he knew nothing of her feelings for Tristan. It was bewildering and very unpleasant to be spoken to like this, the more so when it could achieve nothing. If Tristan hoped to come to court and make a wealthy marriage that was his business, and could make no difference at all to Kate who knew she had no hold on him. The only possible effect on her would be to make her wish to avoid any contact with the court for fear they should chance to meet.

She realised then that Marguerite had fallen silent at last, the waspish stream of gossip at an end. Relieved, Kate said quickly: 'Good day, madame,' and dropped a very small curtsy, and turned to go.

'Wait!' came the command. She turned her expression matching that of the Marquise for haughtiness. 'I did not say I had finished with you. You do not go until I say so.' Kate paused, head high, eyes defiant. The Marquise, perhaps admitting defeat, said coldly: 'You may go.' And watched as Kate mounted her horse unaided, all supple grace and quick agile movement; and then rode away into the sunlight. 'The devil take the girl!' thought Marguerite venomously. 'Why did she not go home to be married like any normal young woman? I hope at least that after today she'll make herself scarce.'

Kate, bubbling with inward rage, rode without thought into the trees, taking the first path that opened before her. Her only impulse was to put as great a distance as possible between herself and the horrible woman she had just left. She felt as if she could scarcely breathe, as if she needed some clearer, purer air to drive out the contamination of that brief contact with the Marquise. Even her thoughts of Tristan were tainted now by her knowledge that this was the woman who had made him what he was. 'I should have married William,' she thought suddenly. 'At least he is exactly as he seems.' And then she began to cry.

By some miracle she did not lose herself in the forest, although she rode for hours without any thought for where she was going. She found when she came to her senses at last that she had in fact ridden full circle, and made her way, without knowing it, back to the château. She had no appetite for supper that night, and excused herself and went straight to bed.

Twelve

The next day Kate found herself for a short time attending alone on Queen Mary, with only the young Princess Louise Marie, a child of four, to overhear their talk. Kate, busy with some hated embroidery, waited until the little Princess had become absorbed in undressing her rag doll before she said to the Queen: 'Madame, you have been very good to me – but I think it is time I thought of leaving St Germain.'

The Queen raised her black eyebrows.

'Indeed, my dear Katherine, I know you made no secret that you did not wish to stay here for ever, but why do you wish to go so soon? Where will you go?'

Kate bent her head.

'That's the trouble – I don't know. I only know I wish to go.' She began to wish that she had not, after all, brought the subject up. Now the Queen would be sure to ask why she had made this sudden decision, and she could think of no acceptable answer. She could not say: 'Because I fear that one day, here or at Versailles, I may meet Marguerite de Tacoignières again – or, worse still, Tristan himself.' Yet it was yesterday's encounter which had driven her to this decision.

She knew that the Queen's dark eyes were resting on her face, studying her expression, but she did not look up. There was a little silence, and then Queen Mary said gently: 'You refused a good marriage, and stayed here though you did not wish to do so. I have watched you often. Is it an affair of the heart?'

Kate, startled, looked up quickly, her colour rising, and tried to stammer out some kind of reply without quite knowing what she was saying. The Queen smiled.

'Someone perhaps whom you do not wish to meet?' she added. She raised a hand as Kate tried again to speak. 'There is no need to say anything, whether I am right or not. You wish to go, and if you are sure, that is enough. But you are single and friendless and have no fortune to take with you, whatever your prospects may be. I will of course help you in any way I can if it is within my power. Do you think perhaps of a convent?'

It was the usual solution for a girl crossed in love, or with no other future open to her, but Kate looked dismayed.

'I ... I have no vocation, madame,' she faltered. For the Queen that was objection enough. She took the matter of a vocation very seriously. After all, had she not been sure herself from her earliest years that she was called to be a nun, so much so that it had taken the intervention of the Pope himself to force her out of the convent where she had entered happily upon her novitiate, and into marriage with the widowed King James? The marriage was, now, a very happy one, but in the circumstances Queen Mary could never look on a convent as an appropriate last resort for an unmarried girl. She smiled now. 'So–' she said. 'What then? You must have given it some thought.'

Kate had, but without coming to any very helpful conclusion.

'Do you think someone might want a governess?' she suggested.

'It is possible. To serve as a governess to some noble family is not a disgrace – but it can be very hard, and without thanks at the end. However, you are, I know, fond of children–' She glanced at her small daughter, and remembered how happily Kate played with her and, when his lessons permitted, with her elder brother Prince James;

and then she said: 'If you wish I shall make enquiries – though I can promise nothing.'

Kate thanked her warmly. The interview did not, however, as she had hoped, spare her a forthcoming visit to Versailles. During the whole period of their stay – almost a week long – she was tormented by the fear that she might come face to face with Tristan, and the certainty of another confrontation with Marguerite. Yet, as it happened, she saw neither of them. She did, however, return to St Germain with a number of very clear impressions of Versailles, and some decided opinions as a consequence.

'I think,' she said to Harry as they sat at supper together a few days later: she had a free evening, 'I think that King Louis's court is corrupt in the extreme.'

Harry glanced round quickly, as if he feared that the woodwork might conceal some lurking eavesdropper. Then he protested vehemently: 'That's a terrible thing to say! Oh, maybe once there were goings on – the sort of things you might find in any court. When Madame de Montespan was the King's mistress, for instance – but that was a long time ago. Now that Madame de Maintenon sets the tone it's quite different – you yourself said how dull you find it.

'That's not what I meant,' explained Kate. 'It's dull here too – even more dull – but not like that. I know I complain sometimes that they do nothing here but go to church, and that all the piety is stifling, but at least they have their hearts in the right place. At Versailles, they make a show of worshipping God, and I know Madame de Maintenon's a model of piety, but in reality it's the King they worship.' Harry looked shocked. He was, surprisingly, perhaps, not yet too drunk to register emotion. 'Oh yes,' Kate went on, unrepentant, 'he's their idol – he's all anyone ever thinks of. Every man and woman in that place spends every moment of every day trying to win his favour, flattering and fawning, so that I don't suppose he's heard an honest opinion on anything in years, from anyone. Nothing at all is ever done without putting him first. Everything revolves round him.'

'And why not?' demanded Harry. 'Look what he's done for France – look at Versailles – look at how half Europe fears him–'

'And how France is nearly bled white by wars,' Kate reminded him. 'Why else is he making peace with King William, whom he hates? He has no choice.'

'It won't last,' said Harry airily. 'You'll see.

It's just to give him a breathing space. And you know, Kate,' he added, suddenly confiding, 'I think if only King James, or his brother, or better still his father, had acted like King Louis has then he'd be King still. King Louis learned a wise lesson from all the unrest in the country when he was a boy. He learned that too powerful nobles and a weak King make for trouble – so now he has all the powerful men at court waiting on his every word, dependent on him for everything, and he's made it all so splendid they all want to have a part in it. France is stronger and more united now than she has ever been. He's made the throne safe for his descendants for generations to come.'

Kate looked sceptical.

'And what of the peasants living in poverty because the landowners must have every penny to spend at court? And the land neglected, and trade despised, and the too-burdensome taxes, and all the rest of it?'

'What do you know about such things?' Harry asked in surprise. 'Leave that to the King and his council – they know what they're doing. It's not a matter for a woman – don't worry your pretty head about it.'

Kate opened her mouth indignantly, and then shut it again. What was the point? The old Harry would, she was sure, never have spoken to her like that; but then the old Harry had gone for good. Suddenly depressed, she began instead to talk of the prospects for the next day's hunting.

Kate's only moments of real pleasure these days were spent in the forest. That first ride alone, when, despite her distraught state, she had come home safely afterwards, had given her confidence in her own sense of direction. Often when her duties freed her she would set off on horseback, unescorted, and ride for hours under the trees, the heaped leaves softening her horse's hoofbeats, the frosty air cold on her face, the peace and tranquillity calming her troubled nerves. She was careful though always to go the same way, following her own chosen landmarks, so that she could be sure not to lose herself in the miles of untamed forest. Harry had tried more than once to convince her that she was foolish to ride alone as she did. Her certainty that she would not lose her way did not reassure him at all. There were, he pointed out, other dangers in the forest, not least of them the possibility of meeting a wild boar, with no armed man at one's side for protection. Kate merely laughed at his fears, and told him that her horse could outrun a boar, should the need arise. She did not take his fears seriously, and had in fact come across no trace of any kind of boar or other threatening animal. Once or twice she had thought she heard the sound of hoofbeats somewhere not far away, and that had frightened her much more. A lone man on horseback was likely to be far more of a threat to a solitary female rider than any animal. But very likely the distant rider was as eager as she to be alone, for she caught no sight of him.

She knew that she needed the outlet offered by her rides more and more these days. As the weeks passed, and autumn turned to winter, she did not find she was able to think less often of Tristan de Plouvinel, or cease to care that he would never be hers. On the contrary, the pain grew worse, as if time and absence fed it somehow. Yet that ought not to be the case, she was sure. Time, she had always been told, was a great healer. Soon, surely, the heartache must grow less.

Her greatest hope was that Queen Mary would find her a position as a governess, thus offering her an escape from this way of life which brought her daily reminders of the man she loved. Then indeed, busy with the demanding care of someone else's children, she could not help but give less time to thinking of Tristan, remembering the past, the beloved gestures and mannerisms, the talk, the laughter. But the weeks passed, and the Queen said nothing to her, and Kate began to wonder if she had completely forgotten the matter. She did not quite like to remind her royal mistress: after all, it must seem a very trivial matter to her.

Heavy-hearted, she performed her daily duties as best she cold, trying very hard to be patient. And trying also to still the little voice in her head which whispered ever more frequently to her: 'You should have married William.'

She even found herself sometimes thinking at some length of the man she had rejected: his stolid kindliness, his grave common sense. They were right, she thought, all those people who said I could have done much worse than to marry him. Now that she believed that nothing could make her forget Tristan de Plouvinel she could see that it might well have been as wise a choice as any other. Wiser, perhaps, for she might very soon have had children to love and care for, her own children, so much beloved that she might be able sometimes to endure the thought that their father was not the man she loved.

But there was no point in regretting past decisions. She had made her choice, and she must live with it, for good or ill. Surely, in time, there would be some way out for her, some escape from the present scarcely bearable existence?

A few days before Christmas she was returning at dusk from one of her customary rides, ambling absent-mindedly along the familiar track towards the long straight drive which led to the château. She was, as so often, deep in thought, scarcely aware of her surroundings, of the now dark shadows beneath the trees, the low slanting shafts of sunlight reaching briefly and furtively into some wide glade, and as quickly shut out when the trees closed in again. It was some time before she realised that another rider was coming towards her. He was almost on her before she saw him, and she drew rein sharply, a little to one side of the track, waiting with fast beating heart for him to reach her. She thought of the unknown rider she had heard sometimes, and was suddenly afraid.

The approaching horseman was a square-set figure on a big-boned horse, and in full daylight might perhaps have looked harmless enough. But in the dim light it was not possible to make out his features, or distinguish anything but the purposeful solidity of his outline. Kate hoped against hope that he would not see her where she sat very still in the partial concealment of the trees.

But he had already seen her, of course, and he drew rein a short way off, and reached up to remove his hat in greeting.

'They said I might find you here,' he said quietly in English. It was an English unaccented, correct, spoken by a man who had known no other tongue. And the slow deliberate tones were teasingly familiar, and yet utterly unexpected. Kate knew that it was a very long time since she had heard that voice. Then he said, with just a hint of uncertainty, as if he was beginning to doubt his own eyes: 'Katherine–'

She knew him then, but even so she could not quite believe what her senses told her. For was he not now a part of her past, over, put behind her for ever?

'William?' she said, in a voice that matched his for hesitancy. 'Is it William?' She peered into the dimness, trying to be sure.

'Of course – who else could it be?'

Kate said nothing, staring at him in bewildered astonishment. She had thought she would never see him again, and yet here he was, facing her in the forest where she rode to forget the past. Or had she imagined him, so caught up in her doubts and uncertainties that her thoughts had conjured him up, as if his presence might somehow help to set her mind at rest?

'It's getting dark, Katherine. It is not very wise of you to be riding here alone. Let us go on our way.'

That sounded like the real William, masterful, conventional, and able to set her nerves tingling with irritation in a way she had almost forgotten until now. She shook off her numbed amazement, and asked sharply: 'What are you doing here?'

'I will explain as we go,' William replied with unruffled dignity. Mechanically, Kate urged her horse forward and they began to ride slowly side by side back towards the château. As they did so, her mind searched frantically through her jumbled impressions for some clue to William's sudden presence here. One possibility made her exclaim suddenly: 'Didn't you get my letter?'

He turned to glance at her.

'Yes, of course.' There was a little pause, as if he were considering his words: William never spoke on impulse. Then he said: 'That is precisely why I came.'

'Oh!'

'Yes – you see, I wanted to make sure that you meant what you said – and that you were well and not in trouble. You did not explain very well why you wished to end our engagement.'

Kate felt her heart beating faster with anxiety.

'I thought I made it very clear,' she said.

'Not to me. I wished to see you, and discuss the whole matter with you.'

Kate remembered now how meticulous William was in everything he did. She should have known that a simple letter would never have been enough to bring matters to an end between them. She wondered now if he had taken any of it seriously at all.

Her next sensation was one of astonishment that he should have come all this way to see her, and that in winter time when a sea crossing must have been difficult in the extreme. It said more than any words for the depth of his feelings for her, and moved her enormously. It astonished her too, for it contradicted all she had ever assumed about his character. She had thought she knew him. But the William she knew would not so have abandoned all prudence and common sense as to undertake the reckless journey which had brought him here. And it was all for her, who had so lightly cast him off. She might love Tristan dc Plouvinel as she could never love this man, but an affection as warm and deep as William's must be for her was worthy of more consideration than that. Perhaps after all she had been rash, and hasty.

There was an interval of silence, and then William said carefully: 'They told me – that is, your brother told me – that you were well. I trust that means that you suffered neither indignity nor hurt at the hands of that barbarous pirate who took you prisoner.'

The words 'barbarous pirate' were said with such venom that Kate was astonished. Once again William was showing a depth of feeling of which she had not thought him capable. But she felt a pang of dismay that he should use such words of Tristan, and found herself on the verge of protesting, and telling him that her captor had not been like that at all. And then she decided that she could not begin to make William understand, and said instead: 'I was very well cared for, thank you. I have no complaints.'

William studied her face as well as he could in the fading light, and then said gravely: 'Your brother led me to understand also that you did not remain here from devotion to the Jacobite cause. I think I have a right to know in that case why you wrote to me as you did, and to hear your decision from your own lips, if indeed it still holds.'

Kate frowned, trying very hard to order her thoughts and to find the right words for her reply. It would be easier, she reflected ruefully, if she knew what that reply was to be. But for the first time since her capture she was not sure. William's coming like this had unsettled all her certainty. It was as if he had come in answer to her niggling doubts about her decision, and by coming had offered her a chance to change her mind, should she wish to take it. And she did not know any longer what she wanted to do.

Instinctively she knew, however, that it would be cruel of her to give William any cause to hope she had changed her mind if there was a chance that she might then revert to her original decision. She could not play around with his feelings so heartlessly. On the other hand, when he had come so far to see her she could not bring herself to send him away at once with an abrupt refusal.

'I'm sorry,' she said at last, very gently, 'but you've taken me by surprise coming suddenly like this. Let's discuss it tomorrow. Are you staying at St Germain tonight?'

'I have found a lodging in the town, with the kind help of your brother. I am invited to supper at the château this evening.'

Harry, Kate recognised, was doing all he could to encourage William. She knew that nothing would please him better than to see the engagement resumed. But she could not change her life simply to please Harry.

At supper Kate found herself seated beside William, though at whose bidding she did not know. Mindful of her wishes, he carefully avoided the matter which had brought him to France, and engaged her in general conversation. This was the old William she remembered only too well, long-winded, slow, precise, and interested in nothing which could capture her enthusiasm or her delight. She felt the familiar, if long-forgotten, sensations creeping over her: a rigid boredom, an almost overwhelming desire to interrupt, jump about, say something appallingly ill-mannered or shocking, anything to break the tedium. Instead, as always, she sat very still staring vaguely about her with a fixed smile giving her face an expression of polite attentiveness. Once only was she jolted out of her boredom, and that was when she caught a brief glimpse of the look on the face of William's other neighbour, Jane Bradfield, another of Queen Mary's ladies. This quiet shy girl was listening to William's talk with such a rapt expression that Kate was astonished. Clearly not everyone found Mr Harwood as tedious as she did. She forced herself to pay closer attention, in case there was some element of William's talk which until now she had missed. After all, on one occasion she had even found Tristan's conversation boring, but he had not then been trying to entertain her, as presumably William was, and she knew that Tristan was capable of being the most delightful of companions. Not once in their acquaintance could she remember having been even mildly interested by William's talk.

She went to bed that night with the dismal conviction that whatever William's devotion to her – and it seemed to be stronger than she had suspected – she could not endure a lifetime of his company. Yet it would be so much easier to be able to tell him tomorrow that she had changed her mind and would marry him after all. It would solve everything. Perhaps, she told herself as she drifted into sleep, she would find William better company in the morning.

He came to the château early, and they walked together in the frosty garden, where at this time of year they could be almost sure of being alone.

'Now,' said William decisively, as soon as they were out of sight of the château, 'you have had time for reflection. What is your answer? Do you hold to your refusal to marry me? I have told no one of your letter except to say that it informed me of your whereabouts. So you see you can so very easily change your mind.'

Kate stood still, clearing a little space in the gravel with her toe, and frowning.

'You make it very hard for me.'

'I thought I made it easy. Or do you mean by that to imply that you intend still to refuse me? I … I care for you very much, you know.' He reddened a little. 'I should do my best to make you happy.'

She looked up at him.

'I'm sure you would. But I doubt if I could make you happy,' she returned candidly. 'You see, I am not much like you. I like excitement, adventure – and I like to be busy–'

'You will have a household to run, servants, perhaps children in time. There will be our neighbours to be entertained–'

Men and women like William, thought

Kate dejectedly, who talked as he did and rarely laughed with the light-hearted joyousness that delighted her. And how could she keep herself fully occupied in a household run by servants, or as a mother of children in the care of a nurse? She had seen how the married women of her acquaintance lived, and she had told herself sometimes that such a life could never satisfy her.

'I don't want to spend my time in needlework and a little gentle music, and instructing the servants. It is not enough. I want to be *useful*–' She looked up at him suddenly. 'Perhaps I can help you with the estate. There must be a great deal to do there.'

William was visibly shocked.

'My dear Katherine, I could not allow that. That would not do at all. A man does not want to marry a business partner. He wants his wife to make his home a welcoming place, where he may return to refresh himself and forget his cares. I am sure you will find a real satisfaction in that– What could be more useful than to create about you a haven for your husband and children? I think of you sometimes seated quietly at my fireside in the evenings, your presence a soothing sweetness at the end of a hard day, your hands busy about some necessary task, your brow unfurrowed with the anxieties that must burden us poor men. Does that not seem to you a very useful part for a wife to play?'

'Perhaps,' thought Kate ruefully, 'if I loved the man – perhaps then it would be bearable. But not if that man is William.' Still she said nothing. After all, he had come all this way to see her; he cared for her, even if he did not appear to know her very well. She could not take that lightly. If only there were some easy solution!

When the silence between them had stretched out for longer than was comfortable, William said: 'Katherine, I thought every woman would be happy to devote her life to the service of the man whom she loved.'

'Possibly,' said Kate, 'I don't know. It has never been asked of me. I am very fond of you, William; but surely you cannot have thought I loved you? It was my relations who arranged it all between us. It was never of my choosing.'

She saw, only too clearly, the hurt in his eyes.

'I thought you consented, at least – and I hoped perhaps, by now, that–'

'That I had come to love you? I'm sorry,

William. It would be wrong of me to pretend. That is why I know I could not settle down quietly to be the kind of wife you want.'

'But you might very well grow to love me in time – that happens very often. You are very young still – you don't yet know what it is to love–'

'Oh, but I do–' she broke in very softly. She saw the surprise on his face, and watched him stare at her, taking in the implications of her words. Then he said:

'So *that* was your reason! There is another man!'

The pain woke, fresh as ever, in her heart.

'That is not all the reason. And he is not a man I can ever marry, or who will ever love me. But I do know what it is to love, and I suppose that is what makes it impossible for me to give my life to you.'

'You do not think you could– Perhaps I could help you forget–'

Kate shook her head, quite sure at last.

'No, William. I am sorry, but I know it would be wrong for me to marry you, or to marry anyone just at the moment–'

'Then you might one day, if I were to ask you again–?'

'No, never. I'm sure of that.' Full of pity

for the fading hope in his eyes, she took his hands in hers. 'I value your friendship most highly – I am grateful that you cared so much as to come all this way to see me – and very moved too. But you have my answer now, and that must be the end of it. I think eventually that you will thank me for it.'

He made a non-committal grunting sound which told her how little he believed her, but he accepted all the same that her decision was made. Kate was sorry that he could not then and there have ridden away, but he had been invited to dinner, and could not without discourtesy fail to be there; and William was a stickler for courtesy. Kate made sure at least that this time she sat as far from him as possible. For his sake she was glad that Jane Bradfield was again his companion, and appeared to be distracting him very effectively from the heartache of the morning. Whenever Kate looked their way they were deeply absorbed in conversation.

William did not seek her out to say good-bye. She was glad of it, and glad too that the Queen kept her busy at some task in the royal apartments for the rest of that day. The next morning she was utterly astonished to see William, whom she had supposed to be

241

by now well on his way back to Ireland, walking in the courtyard with Jane Bradfield. They did not meet, but several times during the next few days she saw him at a distance, and always with the same companion.

After four days he came to where she sat alone at her embroidery and took his seat purposefully at her side. One glance at his face told her more than could any words. She had never seen quite that look on it before, of satisfaction, contentment, a kind of rosy well-being. He looked, she realised startlingly, like a man in love.

'I feel I owe you an explanation,' he began with a smile. 'You must be wondering why I remain here, after our talk the other day. You may perhaps have guessed something of my purpose in remaining, and I would not have you think me fickle or unfeeling.'

Kate let her hands rest unmoving on her lap, and waited for him to go on, for once totally fascinated by what he had to say.

'I realise now that you were quite right when you said we were unsuited to one another. You did me a great favour in ending our betrothal, though I did not think so at the time. I think perhaps I was blinded by some feeling that I thought was love. You have a sparkle, a liveliness which is so very charming that it might make any man think he was in love with you, without reflecting on what kind of woman lies beneath the charm.' Kate was about to exclaim in indignation at this dubious compliment when he went on hastily: 'Not that I mean to imply that you have faults, any more than we all have. But you were right to think that you were not the wife for me. I think we would have been very unhappy together. And because you loved another, you could see that very well. And now,' he went on with a sudden shy self-consciousness, 'I too have had my eyes opened in just that way.'

Kate, to her chagrin, felt a slight but unmistakable pang of jealousy shoot through her, that he should so quickly and so easily find consolation for his loss of her. And then she repressed it hastily and gave him an encouraging smile.

'So that is why you stayed!'

'Indeed,' he acknowledged, his colour heightened still further. 'I … I have reason to hope that Miss Bradfield returns my feelings – and her family, who lodge in the country some miles away, have invited me to visit them for Christmas.'

Then it was much further advanced than she had guessed! For the second time in his life staid, conventional William had acted with swift impulsiveness – and this time, Kate felt, he could only be commended for doing so. Jane Bradfield was a quiet, retiring, home-loving young woman, poor but well-brought up and accomplished, and she was one of the few court ladies who were not Catholic. It was hard to think of a more suitable wife for William than a girl such as Jane. Her jealousy quite forgotten, Kate said with real warmth: 'I am very happy for you – I hope everything goes as well as it can.'

William beamed.

'I think it will– You see,' he added confidingly, 'we think alike, Miss Bradfield and I. It is as if … as if I had found a kindred spirit, if that does not sound too extravagant.'

It did not, Kate assured him, but as she smiled and wished him well she could not help but think with that familiar dull ache how she too had felt she had found a kindred spirit when she met Tristan. She knew exactly how William must feel, that sense of completeness, of homecoming, of knowing that this at least was right. Only unlike William she knew that this sensation, deep and intense though it was, could be one-sided and hopeless and unfulfilled. She hoped – though she did not say – that this was one lesson

William would never have cause to learn.

They parted friends, and Kate was able to be genuinely glad for him. But William's happiness only underlined for her how very different was her own situation. She wanted more intensely than ever to escape from her present way of life. She had almost found the courage to talk to Queen Mary again, in case that lady had forgotten her promise, when the Queen summoned her and announced that she had at last found a suitable position for her, if she wished still to take it up.

In two days King James and his Queen and court were to go to Versailles to celebrate the New Year. Kate's relief at the chance of a reprieve was unbounded. She listened attentively to what the Queen had to tell her of the wealthy nobleman in the Auvergne who was seeking a governess for his children.

'He is, I understand, a good and devout man,' said the Queen. 'And he cares for every member of his household with great seriousness. There are four young children, and he wishes them to be reared with love and firmness. I think you would be well suited to undertake the task – and I think you will also be happy there.'

'How soon do I go?' Kate asked, full of gratitude.

'Not yet,' said the Queen, and Kate's heart sank. 'Your future employer likes to spend this season close to his family. But in Lent he and his wife will spend time separately in religious establishments. Then – in February – they would like you to come and take up your care of the children. So you may take your pleasures at Versailles this time with a light heart, knowing that they are your last.'

So she was not yet free of the haunting possibility of an unwanted meeting! But she had been fortunate so far: perhaps she might be once again. And then she would be gone, hundreds of miles to the south, far away from Versailles and St Germain and distant Brittany. Until then she had only to be patient.

Kate was familiar already with the hundreds of rules and regulations which governed the routine of life at Versailles. She knew – by hearsay, if not by experience – who must precede whom in entering a room, for instance, or in the performance of some meaningless ritual; how one must speak, or knock upon a door, or behave when the King was present. She knew all about the elaborate ceremonies of the King's *lever* and *coucher*.

She thought of them sometimes as she got up or went to bed, alone and unattended, and wondered what it was like to have a ritual for every garment one put on or took off, or even for the more basic and personal functions involved in making ready to face the day. It never ceased to amaze her that one man could demand that these ceremonies should take place with himself at the centre of them. Even less could she understand how so many grown men and women could give all their time and attention to achieving the tiniest favour. One word from the King was a jewel to be treasured and paraded before the court. A denial of precedence, another man achieving the coveted favour, and one would have a deadly quarrel. Children, Kate mused, were often a good deal less childish than adults. It was a strange and alien world. And she had to remind herself, for her own good, that within it she was the outsider and Tristan de Plouvinel was – when there – entirely at home. It served to bring home to her how far removed from her he was. If she had thought them close once, it had been an illusion. This was his world, this and the bloodstained ship he captained, and she could be a part of neither, nor would she wish to be.

The days passed, slowly, with the inevitable hours spent waiting on the King's every move. Once or twice Kate caught a glimpse of Marguerite de Tacoignières, but she neither looked her way nor spoke. Perhaps she thought it was, now, beneath her dignity to acknowledge the existence of so lowly a mortal as Kate.

The last evening came. 'At last!' thought Kate, '–tomorrow we go back to St Germain and then, very soon, I shall go south to a new life, and all this will be behind me!'

Today was one of those set aside for what at Versailles was termed an *apartement*, when King Louis gave what was, for his court, an informal entertainment. The evening began with a concert, and the music was, Kate had to acknowledge, both beautiful and exquisitely performed. As a patron of the arts the King was certainly a success.

After the music, card tables were brought out, and the courtiers flocked to play. Kate was quite sure that many of them had no interest in cards at all, but one was not permitted to sit unless one was playing, so their enthusiasm was understandable. After a day of standing and walking about the court, Kate's own legs ached intolerably, but she could not bring herself to join one or other of the tables where courtiers and their ladies were playing for dizzyingly high stakes. She could not afford to, of course, but then neither could many of the players. But for her also there were too many memories linked with the noisy vigorous games going on around her. It was bad enough to stand by and look on – close by, she realised, two men were playing at lansquenet, the very game she had played day after day in the house of many windows at St Malo.

She felt all at once a steadily growing conviction that she was being observed. She looked up, and there far across the room caught sight of the puppet figure of Marguerite de Tacoignières, although the Marquise was not in fact looking at her. At this distance it was almost possible to believe that she was beautiful. She had enough men about her–

One of them, towering over the rest, his black head bent, was the one man who was never out of her thoughts, and whom she had feared all these months to meet.

She began, to her shame, to tremble violently. High-coloured, weak at the knees, she looked about frantically for some means of support. There was an empty chair nearby, but she dared not sit down. Instead, she clasped the back, leaning her weight on it as discreetly as she could. 'I wish I could go home,' she thought miserably. But where was home? Her room here at Versailles? Her lodging at St Germain? That unknown château in the Auvergne? There was nowhere else, yet home was an empty word if that was all it meant.

She glanced across the room again. He was talking animatedly now, gesticulating in the way she knew so well, and loved so much. Marguerite was standing listening in a kind of frozen stillness; but then if she were to show any emotion that enamelled surface would crack, or so Kate thought. Slowly, carefully, she edged herself back to a corner where the candlelight was just a little less bright and a heavy velvet curtain offered her a measure of concealment.

The brown hands rose in a lavish gesture of finality, and Tristan bowed crisply and turned away from the Marquise. Something in the briskness of his manner suggested anger. Kate watched, fearful of being seen yet hungry to miss nothing. And then she was sure he looked her way.

She shrank back and bent her head, so that the jostling courtiers in the room should hide her from view. How much longer would the card playing go on? Surely it must all be over soon. She dared not even look about for Harry or any of the other guests from St Germain, for fear that her eyes should be drawn yet again to that tall beloved figure.

And then all at once there was a little stir in the crowd near her; a pause; and a hand was laid on her arm.

'Miss Kate–'

That deep wonderful voice! She had forgotten how attractive it was, and how alluring her name sounded in his oddly accented English. She turned, holding tight to the curtain for the support it could give – her legs seemed to have no power at all – and looked up into those dark eyes that had, so often, haunted her dreams.

'Oh!' she cried breathlessly. 'You're back from sea then.' She was furious with herself for being so unable to think of anything intelligent to say. She wondered if he was offended at her lack of finesse, for he did not smile.

'Yes,' he said. 'And you are still in France.'

There was a silence, during which she tried frantically to think of something to say. Otherwise he might go away, and painful and tormenting though this meeting was

251

she did not want it to end – or not like this, at least, in an aura of awkwardness and embarrassment.

'Will you play at cards?'

She stared at him, as if he had asked something impossible. How could she play here, in an atmosphere and a place so different from that where they had played before? Even if she had the money – but she knew that it would be a terrible breach of etiquette to admit to having no means for gambling. She shook her head.

'No thank you,' she said stiffly. She looked up at him with a hint of a smile. 'I'm told you can't sit down unless you're playing.'

'That's so– Do you wish to sit down?'

Some mischievous sprite inside her head urged her to reply 'Not if you hold me in your arms – then I shall not be tired.' But she said only: 'Yes, I should like to.'

He did not offer her a seat, but then presumably it was not in his power to do so. Only the King could do that, and there was not the remotest chance that he would so break with convention as to do so for a penniless English girl.

'Never mind,' said Tristan consolingly. 'This will soon be over. It is nearly ten o'clock– Tell me, when–?' What he had been about to ask she was never to know, for a cold voice broke suddenly in upon them. In her total absorption in Tristan's company, Kate had not seen Marguerite de Tacoignières coming their way.

'Monsieur le Comte de Plouvinel,' she said, laying a hand on his arm with chilly playfulness, 'you are neglecting your devoted friends. You cannot be so heartless! Come, let us enjoy a round or two of ombre–'

Kate thought, watching him, that if Tristan were ever to look at her as he looked now at Marguerite, she would shrivel away to ashes where she stood.

'I told you I had no wish to play,' he said incisively, turning pointedly back to Kate. Somewhere beneath the painted surface a natural colour spread across Marguerite's face. For a moment her eyes sparkled with a light which hinted at the beauty she must once have had.

'So you play games of another kind instead,' she snapped. 'But have a care – this game is dangerous.'

Tristan glanced at her, eyebrows raised.

'Indeed?' Her hand closed more firmly about his arm.

'I meant only that you are in danger of neglecting your old and trusted friends for those in whom you can have no such confidence,' she said coaxingly. 'What is more the King himself wishes for your company. Would you deny him too?'

Tristan looked across the room to where, now, King Louis was indeed standing, talking to the men who had formed part of Marguerite's entourage. It was possible that his presence there had no connection with Marguerite, and that he was not even aware that she and Tristan were in the room, but if he had expressed a wish for the company of the Comte de Plouvinel, then only a very foolish man, blind to his own interests, would risk a refusal. Tristan was not a foolish man, and he bowed curtly to Kate, offered his arm to Marguerite and led her back across the room towards the waiting monarch.

Kate, shivering suddenly in the draught from the open window behind her, watched him go. He had not behaved towards Marguerite like a man in love. In fact his manner had suggested hatred more than any other emotion. Yet clearly the Marquise still had some kind of power over him, for she had succeeded in taking him from Kate's side, which was, Kate supposed, exactly what she had intended to do. And as for Tristan, had it been anything other than stubbornness, and a dislike for being ordered around by this powerful woman, that had made him wish to stay with Kate? Perhaps she would never know, for tomorrow she would go back to St Germain, and very soon to the Auvergne, and it was unlikely that her path would ever cross with that of Tristan de Plouvinel again. She was glad when, shortly afterwards, the *apartement* came to an end and she was able at last to go to bed.

Marguerite de Tacoignières did not go to bed, even when she was dressed in her silken nightgown, with a frilled hood covering her hair, and her maid had been dismissed. She sat for a long time at her ornate and gilded dressing table, gazing into the mirror and seeing, not the ageing woman pictured there, but some other darker vision which set her lips in a hard line and drew her finely pencilled brows together in a frown. It was close to midnight when at last she stirred, and rang for a servant, and instructed him to carry out an errand of great urgency. Yet even riding through the night at full speed, the man did not reach the poor lodging house in one of the less reputable areas of Paris until after dawn. Perhaps the warmth of his welcome was adequate compensation for a sleepless night. Certainly the fair scarred man who received him had been waiting a very long time for just this summons, and had by now almost given up hope that it would ever come.

Thirteen

It was a relief to Kate to return to St Germain: a relief, and yet a pain, for that uncomfortable meeting with Tristan had only served to remind her how much she loved him. Not that she needed reminding. It was the forgetting that was hard, for he had never been absent from her thoughts for more than a few minutes together since she had first set eyes on him. Now she wondered how she could ever have imagined that the trivial distractions of court life could quench the devouring flame that consumed her. It would be like trying to dampen the fires of a volcano with a cup of water – a pointless exercise. She could of course make a new life for herself, and must do so, but she knew now that if she wandered the world in search of adventure she would find nothing to bring forgetfulness or rid her of her love.

Queen Mary observed with concern that she looked tired, and gave her an afternoon to herself.

257

'I always find Versailles very tiring myself,' she commented sympathetically. Kate wondered if she guessed at the reason for her companion's careworn look, but she simply accepted her free time with gratitude, and made arrangements to ride in the forest.

It was a day of crisp sunshine and frost, the kind of day she would once have found exhilarating. Even in her present frame of mind she took some comfort from the cold air and the brightness of the sun. But it would take more than a fine day to bring her real consolation. As she rode slowly along the familiar track her mind was full of crowding memories, of last night above all – though already it seemed much longer ago than that.

If only, she thought, she had not been so overwhelmed by the shock of seeing him, then she might have been able to talk coherently, even to question him. She could, for instance, have asked him how he had fared at sea; or what he intended to do now. But perhaps that would have brought her too close to the question she could never have asked: was he indeed looking for a rich wife? However much she loved him, it did not give her the right to ask that. But she would have liked to know the answer. On the other hand, perhaps she knew it already, but would rather pretend she did not. After all, Marguerite de Tacoignières was a widow, influential and extremely wealthy. She had known Tristan for a long time, had almost certainly been his mistress, and perhaps had known that until now he had not seriously considered marriage. He was too happy in his carefree way of life to tie himself to a woman. But if Marguerite was right that was about to change. And it was only too likely that the Marquise wanted him. She could not hope to lure him with beauty and charm, so in its place wealth and birth would have to do. Would he be tempted? Kate wondered. He had not behaved towards her like a man planning marriage. But then any marriage he made would be a matter of cold calculation, not of affection or attraction. And if Marguerite wanted him, she would do all in her power to lay hands on this great prize.

It was hardly surprising that she should want him so much, thought Kate ruefully. One had only to look at him to be drawn irresistibly by that powerful physical presence. His great height marked him out, of course, as it had last night from the far side of the room; but it was not that alone. He carried himself with such arrogant grace, so that every movement was a joy to watch: the supple strength of his limbs and his body as he walked and stood and sat, the hint of danger when he was startled into alertness, the expressive fluency of his hands as he talked, the poise of his head beneath its heavy shining crown of dark curls. And then when he was close, standing so very near, looking down – then the attraction was so strong as to be almost unbearable. The lines of his dark face filled her mind now in memory, hard lines, windbeaten and tanned, yet with the laughter lines to soften the bright eyes, the long lavish curve of the thick lashes, the mouth that could part in a smile so dazzlingly sweet that even thinking of it she could scarcely breathe–

Her eyes misted with tears, she tightened her fingers about the rein, the nails digging into her palms as if she might somehow drive out the agony in her heart with simple physical pain. Her horse, sensing her distress, shied uneasily; and the next moment stumbled, tried to right himself, and stumbled again, rolling to the ground. Kate gave a cry, pulled at the reins, and found herself thrown high and clear to land on the leaves beyond him.

She sat up, rubbing her head, shaken but

unhurt. The horse was already struggling to his feet. 'Poor old boy,' she murmured, 'all because I–' And then all at once she was thrust forward on her face in the leaves, and someone was binding her hands behind her with ruthless efficiency, and before she had time to struggle or to cry out her eyes were blindfolded and an evil smelling rag dragged across her mouth, gagging her.

She was dragged to her feet, and a furious kick only brought a blow in response. Someone gave her a shove, and then hands on either side pulled her roughly with them through the trees. She knew there must be at least two men – always supposing they were men – but they worked silently, so she had no sounds to guide her.

They walked what seemed a long way, until the harsh dragging of branches and brambles at her clothes and hair told her they were taking a little-used path – if it was a path at all, and not simply one of the dense thickets which dotted the forest here and there. Beyond it was some kind of building, for she heard steps on stone a moment before her own feet found some hard flat surface beneath them. A door opened and closed, with a noise that suggested long disuse, and a damp chillness wrapped her round. The next moment gag and blindfold were removed, and she found herself looking into the fair shifty face she thought had gone from her life for ever.

'Hervé!' Terror shot through her. Better far to have found herself faced with a stranger, than this man whose desperate ruthlessness she knew only too well. 'Why?' she asked herself quickly. 'What can he hope to gain this time?' Since no answer came to mind, she swallowed hard and tried to give an appearance of calmness. She looked round her at the four damp green-stained stone walls, the unsound roof, the only-too-adequate door. Perhaps this place had been built as some kind of temporary shelter for huntsmen in the forest. She could not tell. It was not in any case very welcoming now.

'There is no escape, as you see,' said Hervé, as her gaze returned unwillingly to him. Kate swallowed again.

'How … what… You frightened my horse, I suppose?'

Hervé nodded.

'The oldest trick there is, mademoiselle – the hidden rope in the path.'

'But – how could you know I would come this way?'

Hervé smiled slightly.

'You always come this way,' he said simply. 'You have been watched.'

Kate shivered. 'By you?'

'No – by another – or perhaps more than one. I don't know.'

Kate had a sudden horrible sense of being surrounded by a multitude of unknown enemies. She linked her fingers tightly together, as far as her bound hands would allow, and asked as steadily as she could: 'But why? What have I done–?'

Hervé shrugged. 'Nothing, as I can tell. But there is a man who has done me great wrong, as I think you know. Me, and others, who are my friends–'

Slowly his meaning reached Kate. He must mean Tristan – yet she had no links now with Tristan.

'What do you mean to do? I have nothing to do with – that man.'

'No? We shall see.' He began to turn away, but she burst out indignantly: 'Don't you remember how generous he was to you? He let you go free, after all you'd done. How can you want to harm him?'

Hervé turned back to her, his face livid with hate. And then with slow deliberation, he spat on the floor at Kate's feet.

'That is what I think of his generosity! Oh

yes, he let me go free, like a schoolboy caught stealing sweets – or like a peasant! It wouldn't do, would it, to raise his noble sword to someone as far beneath him as I am? A fair fight with low-born Hervé – that would never do. He might soil his fine noble blade with unworthy blood. And of course being a man of honour – or wanting to look like one in front of a lady – he can't just kill a defenceless man. So he has to let me go. I'm carrion anyway, beneath his contempt– Well, now he'll learn the truth, and for once I'll have the pleasure of seeing his high and mightiness grovelling in the dust for mercy.'

Was it true? thought Kate painfully. Was it possible that Tristan had not been moved by generosity at all, but by contempt? It had not seemed like it at the time, but looking back she could not be sure. And Hervé himself was so very sure, the anger and resentment pouring out, feeding the long cherished hatred of the man who for so long had been his Captain.

But whether it was true or not she was sure of one thing: Tristan now was in deadly danger, and somehow she was to be the means to bring him down.

'It's me you have prisoner, not him,' she reminded Hervé. 'And I'm nothing to him now. There's no one who'll pay a ransom for me.'

'Oh yes there is – but the ransom will be death. Only he will not know that until he comes.'

'You're mad!' Kate exclaimed. 'I tell you, he's not interested in me any more. You know so much – don't you realise I'm not betrothed any more? – and my brother's a poor man – there's no one who'll pay to set me free.'

'He will pay,' he said with utter conviction. 'He will pay with his life.'

Kate stared at him, feeling sick, but unable to think of anything to say. After a moment Hervé turned aside and took something from a saddle bag lying on the floor in a corner.

'Here,' he said. 'You are going to write a letter.' He held out paper, pen and ink. When she made no move to take them, but simply continued to gaze at him, he seemed about to grow angry. And then he remembered something. 'Ah, of course – your hands are tied!' He laid down the writing materials and came behind her, knife in hand. 'Don't try anything,' he warned. 'There are eight men outside, concealed but armed and watchful. One cry from me and they will come – and they have orders to kill if need be, even so

265

soon as this.' Kate felt the ropes fall from her wrists, and drew her hands forward, rubbing where the bonds had chafed the skin. 'Now,' said Hervé, 'you will write to the Comte de Plouvinel, as I instruct you.'

'What do you think that will do?' demanded Kate.

'He will come, of course,' said Hervé.

'But he's at Versailles. It will take hours for him to get here, even if he comes, which I doubt. Meanwhile my brother and my friends at St Germain will have grown anxious, and they'll come and search for me.'

'They won't find this place. And in any case it will soon be dark. And they will not search. One of my companions has taken the horse back to St Germain. He has a good story, that you paid him to do so, and to tell your friends that you have run away with the Comte de Plouvinel and will not return.'

Kate coloured angrily.

'They'll never believe that!' But she knew even as she spoke that those who knew her best would be only too likely to believe it, unless they doubted Tristan's part in the matter. But if she knew he was unlikely ever to run away with her, that did not mean that others would know it. It would explain

266

Tristan's absence, too, of course, if he should make a sudden disappearance from Versailles. But of course she had no intention of playing the part Hervé wanted her to play in that.

He was urging the writing materials on her again, but she shook her head vehemently. 'No – you can't make me write!'

The knife slid out and she found herself as in Hervé's house, held immovably, with the blade at her throat.

'Can't I?' asked Hervé. 'I shall stand over you – one false move and my blade slips. Now write!' He released her arms.

Her hands trembling, she crouched down on the flagged floor and spread the paper before her, horribly aware of the threatening blade.

'What do you want me to write?'

He thought for a moment, then began slowly to dictate.

'"Monsieur le Comte, I hunger for you with the most burning passion known to woman–"'

Kate sat still, pen poised.

'I can't write that! You can't make me – and it wouldn't bring him anyway!'

'It will – you'll see it will! Write – quickly now, or you'll be dead with hunger and cold

267

before he comes.'

All at once a new possibility occurred to Kate – a way out, if only she dared try it. Hervé was leaning over her, his unsavoury breath hot on her cheek, his eyes on the unmarked surface of the paper before her. Very slowly and deliberately Kate put pen to paper and wrote, in English, 'Hervé means harm–' She paused, waiting for Hervé's furious outburst. But none came. After a moment he merely said impatiently: 'Get on with it! "I hunger for you–"'

Kate, trying to hide her delight, continued to write, steadily, as she had begun: a detailed account of all she knew of the danger that threatened Tristan. Her gamble had paid off: Hervé, quite obviously, could not read.

She signed her name with a flourish and laid down the pen.

'There you are then,' she said with a show of truculence. 'It won't work.'

The knife was put away. Hervé swooped on the paper and folded it triumphantly, and then bound her hands again before taking it to the door and handing it to one of the men outside.

'Pierre will have it at Versailles before dark,' he assured her. Kate tried to look suitably troubled.

And there her luck ended. A few seconds only had passed, when the door was pushed open again and Pierre, red with rage, burst in, waving the offending letter.

'Can't you read, you stupid oaf?' he shouted at Hervé. 'There's not a word you told her to say here – God knows what she's written – it's English, I think. Where would we be if we were all as thick as you?'

Hervé reddened, and then turned to vent his anger on Kate, hitting her sharply across the face.

'Bitch! Sly, scheming bitch! How dare you try to cross me!'

'She'd better write it again,' said Pierre. 'I'll stand over her this time and see she does as she's told.'

Kate clutched at a last faint hope.

'I … I can't write French,' she protested. 'I only speak it.'

'You'll write, never fear,' Pierre told her. 'Even if I have to spell every word– Now get on with it.'

She had no choice. They unbound her and stood over her, one on each side, both armed; and Pierre watched like a hawk for any word which did not echo Hervé's dictation. The finished result pleased him enormously, and he read it aloud with dramatic emphasis.

'Monsieur le Comte, I hunger for you with the most burning passion known to woman. Come to me here in the forest in this lodge which will see the consummation of our union, and I shall be yours for ever. Do not delay – come at once, for I cannot bear that we should be apart for one hour more. Your own, Katherine.'

Beneath the impassioned words which, in other circumstances, she might have found hilariously funny, Kate watched Pierre sketch a careful plan of their hiding place, marking the route that would being Tristan to it. And then he folded the paper and set out on his errand.

When the door had closed behind him, Kate said to Hervé: 'Why don't you believe that a letter like that won't bring him? He's not interested in me.'

'No?' He leered at her unpleasantly, and then came to bind her hands again, touching her suggestively as he did so. 'You're a woman, aren't you? And young and clean and a virgin. And you've a fine dowry lined up – just what a man in need of cash might be looking for. A mite more toothsome than an old hag like Marguerite de Tacoignières too.'

Kate gazed at him disbelievingly. Could

that be why the Marquise had warned her off, and interfered when Tristan had gone out of his way to talk to her? Did she believe that Tristan saw in Kate the rich wife he was seeking? Even with her grandfather's dowry she was hardly that – on the other hand, she had no idea of the value of an English dowry to a Frenchman, or what indeed a Frenchman might regard as an acceptable sum. Was it possible that Tristan, thwarted of her ransom, could be trying to improve his fortunes in this way? That, indeed, he might even wish to marry her?

She sat where she was on the floor, dazed with the effort of trying to understand, overwhelmed by the astonishing thought of marriage to Tristan de Plouvinel. In a moment her world was transformed, her future and all its possibilities. Suddenly, all at once, it was as if she held the universe in her hands, with all its limitless delights at her command. Tristan at her side, her own for ever, her dear love, her husband – it was too much to take in.

And it was not after all the dazzling prospect it seemed. If he wished to marry her, it was not because her love was returned, but because he wanted her money, as coldly as once he had used Marguerite to set him on the first steps of his career at sea. She would be a means to an end, a means to keep him at the court she despised, and in which she was a stranger. Very likely she would be banished to his estates to kick her heels there while he spent her dowry on his clothes and horses and mistresses, and fawned with all those other courtiers on the King at Versailles. 'I could not bear that,' she thought bleakly. 'To be so near to delight, and yet to be shut out. Not when I have seen now and then what treasures are possible for the woman who wins his heart.'

In any case, she reflected after a moment, marriage was not something which would be offered to her even if Hervé was right in every respect. If Tristan did indeed want to lay his hands on her dowry, then that was being used as the lure to draw him here, to certain death at Hervé's hands. Kate could only hope that Hervé was wrong.

She wondered then how he had come to believe that Tristan hoped to marry her, since it was something she had never suspected. Could the Captain have spoken of it to this man who had been his second in command? But no, the break with Hervé had come long ago, before she had decided to end her engagement. It was unlikely that

Hervé had even known of her summons to St Germain. He had spoken then as if he believed her still Tristan's prisoner.

Of course he might have followed them to St Germain or Versailles when they came east, and hung about the courts gathering any crumbs of gossip which came his way. But it was surely very unlikely that any link between herself and Tristan could be the subject of gossip, for they never met, and she had told no one of her feelings. Harry might perhaps have guessed something, but he did not know Tristan at all, except by name and repute. Only Marguerite de Tacoignières was in a position to know anything of Tristan's thought or intentions.

Only Marguerite de Tacoignières–

Marguerite, who had warned her off, and intervened when Tristan showed an interest in her. Marguerite, who had no beauty left with which to lure him to her bed, and must fear that if he married she might lose every hold she had over him. Marguerite, who very likely longed to marry him herself.

Kate looked up at Hervé. Was he in Marguerite's pay, or at least in collusion with her? Tristan had said he had found that Hervé was working against him on behalf of 'an enemy'. Was it possible that the enemy

273

was Marguerite – and that she was using Hervé's hatred of Tristan for her own ends? But why should she do so? If she loved Tristan it was a very odd way to show it.

On the other hand, Kate doubted very much if Marguerite was capable of love. Possessiveness, lust, a wish to control, greed – yes, all those must be a part of her. And all those could make her turn in anger and hatred against the very man she wanted, if it was clear that he had cast her off.

'Is the Marquise de Tacoignières behind all this?' demanded Kate. She thought momentarily that Hervé looked startled. But then he grinned and returned smoothly: 'What if she is? Anyone of sense knows better than to tangle with her.'

So that answered her question, and explained only too well why this had come about. It also made it more than likely that Hervé was right about Tristan, and that he would come, for Marguerite must know better than most what would make him set out in the dark on a perilous ride to some secret rendezvous. In fearful anticipation Kate sat straining her ears for any sound which might tell her he was coming.

As it grew dark – there was only one tiny high barred window, so the light had never been very great – two men from outside came in, and a lantern was lit. They must be expecting Tristan to arrive soon, Kate supposed, and were getting ready to receive him. They crouched in a corner playing cards and drinking from a flask one of them carried. Kate, remembering some of that last unpleasant experience at Hervé's hands, was relieved that he did not drink. Perhaps he wanted to keep his wits about him for Tristan's arrival.

It was bitterly cold in the little room. Kate sat huddled in her cloak, too chilled to sleep, and too afraid. She tried not to think what would happen when Tristan came. Would the five men left outside overpower him the moment he arrived on the scene? Or would Hervé wait until he was safely indoors, right in the heart of the trap set to kill him, for which she was the bait? Kate, shivering, thought that it did not really matter much, for the end would be the same.

She had no idea how many hours had passed when they heard the sound of someone riding at a steady pace along some path not far away. The hoofbeats ceased after a time, and there was a pause, and then the sound of twigs snapping underfoot, and branches being brushed aside. There was a sudden stifled shout, quickly broken off. And then the door opened, and Tristan, stooping under the low sill, came in. Kate watched him with her heart in her mouth, love and pity and fear and a desperate longing to warn him all rising in her together.

But there was nothing she could do. The two men lurking either side of the door grasped his arms, and one kicked the door shut, and they held him to face Hervé across the little lantern lit room. He made no attempt to resist: perhaps he realised that there would be no point. Kate saw his eyes, bright and alert, allowing no fear to show, travel towards her, and back to Hervé again.

'It seems,' he said in a light-hearted tone which reverberated strangely through the tense air of the room, 'that I am not the only one for whom Miss Kate entertains a burning passion. What a woman – one can only hold one's breath and admire!'

Hervé sprang forward and struck him across the mouth with all the force of a man who has been aching for years to do just that.

'Shut up! The time for laughter is over – you are at last about to get what you deserve!'

Fourteen

There was a red mark across Tristan's face, but he did not appear to be aware of it.

'Yes,' he said. 'I gathered that the warmth of the reception meant something. Can I assume that Miss Pendleton did not in fact pen that alluring letter?'

Hervé grinned unpleasantly.

'What do you think?' He turned the smile, triumphant now, on Kate. 'I said he would come, didn't I? She didn't believe you would be interested, you see,' he explained to Tristan. 'But then she didn't know you were after her dowry. Very convenient, her breaking off her betrothal just when you had lost the chance of a ransom–' Kate thought for a moment that a flicker of surprise travelled over Tristan's face, and then was gone. He had not known, then, that her betrothal was at an end.

'What a pity,' Hervé went on, 'that your dream will never be fulfilled. The world will think you have run away together, and it will scarcely have ceased to gossip about it when

277

your bodies will be found, loverlike, together in death, the victims of a devotion which led you wandering in the forest until so deep in love were you that you lost your way, and cold and hunger and the wild animals did the rest. A touching tale, fit for a romance, don't you think?'

Kate shivered: so she was to die too. Hervé had not told her that. For a tiny moment her eyes met Tristan's, and she felt obscurely comforted. I shall be calm and brave, she thought, just as he is.

'Very romantic,' Tristan agreed cheerfully. 'I suppose Marguerite will weep with the rest of them– Let's hope the paint does not run.' Then, suddenly, his tone changed, at once harsh, confident, even threatening. 'But I fear there will be more weeping than you anticipate, my friend. I had hoped to spare your mother, but you were too stupid to take your chance. This time you will not be so fortunate. As for Marguerite, she will weep in truth – the harder because she will not be able to tell anyone why she is weeping without admitting her guilt.'

Kate could see that Hervé was taken aback, his confidence momentarily shaken.

'What do you mean?' he demanded, in a tone which was meant to sound aggressive.

'You thought I'd come alone, didn't you, believing every word of that silly letter? I'm not quite so stupid. I have a score of armed men out there, and your minions in the bushes are by now disarmed and bound.'

'I don't believe you!' Panic sharpened Hervé's tone.

'Don't you? In a moment I shall call out, and this room will be invaded—'

'Then you'll die first!' cried Hervé, and flung himself forward, knife in hand. Kate screamed.

There was an interval of total confusion. Someone knocked over the lantern, and it went out. Kate heard the door burst open, the rush of feet, shouts and cries. She dared not move, pressed against the wall waiting in horror for it all to end. She heard Tristan's voice shouting orders, and prayed that he was unhurt. Then the struggle spilled outside again. Kate heard departing hooves, and riders in pursuit, and more cries further off. The room emptied, and she was alone.

She got up stiffly, and went to the door, cramped and cold, but thankful for the clear air. Had they forgotten her? She would never find her way home without help, bound as she was. She could still hear the crash of feet and hooves in some conflict a little way off, and a sudden pistol shot sharp above the sound of shouting men.

Much later – or so it seemed – someone came back towards her, brushing through the thicket. She shrank back, straining to see in the darkness. The shape of a man loomed up, black and ominous, and she could not force out the words to ask who he was.

'Kate? Miss Kate?'

She wanted to reach out and touch him, but she could not free her hands. She sensed his presence, though, warm and alive in the cold night. Then he passed her and moved away across the room.

'Let us have some light,' he said. She heard him fumble about for lantern and tinder box, and after a while a light leapt up to illuminate his dark face. He looked very stern, and she was reminded of that other time when he had rescued her. Was it to be like that again? But this time he could hardly blame her for what had happened.

He stood up and looked at her.

'You are unhurt, I think,' he said. 'What happened?'

'Aren't you going to untie me?' she asked in her turn, and he apologised briefly and did so, his hands efficient and cool. Then she told him as simply as she could all that had happened, and when she came to the letter he nodded and said, with a ghost of a smile: 'Yes, that warned me. I knew you could not have written like that.'

So she hadn't needed to write in English after all. But did that mean that he did not think it possible that she loved him, or only that he knew she could not express herself like that? Before she could decide whether to ask, he went on: 'Hervé is dead, and the other men taken prisoner. You have nothing to fear from them any more.'

Kate was shivering uncontrollably now. She felt unbearably tired, unable to think clearly, and yet tense and irritable, as if she would not be able to rest even if she were at home, in her own bed, and warm and well fed. She ought to be feeling relieved and happy, but she did not seem able yet to grasp that the nightmare was over. Tristan cupped a hand about her elbow, and she started, and looked up at him as if expecting to find some unaccustomed expression on his face; but he looked simply practical and detached, and his tone when he spoke echoed his appearance. 'Now I shall take you home.'

She allowed him to lead her out to where his horse waited beyond the thicket. He put out the lantern which had lit their path, and then lifted her into the saddle, and mounted behind her. His arms, either side of her, held the reins, but they were hard and unyielding against her body, and he sat very upright so that she dared not sink against him as all her instincts urged her to do. She wished he would say something, but she was too weary herself to be able to think of anything which might encourage him to talk. All his attention seemed to be concentrated on finding a safe path through the shadowed forest, lit only fitfully by a cloud-crossed moon. Once, she thought perhaps she had dozed, for she jerked suddenly fully awake to find that nothing seemed to have changed and they were still making their steady but not very comfortable way along the forest rides.

And then at last the wall that edged the château gardens came in sight. She heard Tristan murmur some relieved recognition of the fact. And she suddenly remembered what Hervé had told her about the return of her horse.

'Oh!' she exclaimed involuntarily. Tristan drew rein.

'What is it?' he asked.

'I'd forgotten,' Kate enlarged, faltering a little, 'Hervé said he'd let them know at St Germain that I'd run away – with you.'

This time his arm closed about her, as if steadying her.

'Oh,' said Tristan, in a tone she could not interpret. He was silent for a moment, digesting the information. 'Perhaps,' he suggested then, 'we should behave accordingly, and return as runaway lovers might.'

A curious mixture of embarrassment, longing and irritation rose in Kate. 'What do you mean?' she demanded sharply.

He paused again, and then said very carefully: 'Hervé was right about one thing.'

'Oh – what was that?'

There was another pause, and when he replied it was in an abrupt, almost angry tone. 'That I wish to marry you.'

Kate sat very still, upright, so that he could touch her as little as possible. She realised after a moment that she was holding her breath, and slowly and carefully released it. She was shivering again, but not because she was any colder. She had even begun to warm up a little. She wished desperately that her mind was clearer, that she was not so exhausted. But she could not help that, and she must allow her instinct to guide her.

'I see,' she said at last, very drily. 'I suppose that's honest anyway.' He seemed to be unperturbed by her tone, for he went on:

'So you see, we shall be married at once, quickly – I can find a priest who is willing, I think, even at this time of night. And then you may return to St Germain without disgrace, as my wife.'

Hervé had been right, and Kate felt a bitter anger rise in her.

'Oh yes,' she burst out harshly. 'All very neat and convenient, isn't it? I've escaped Hervé only to play right into your hands. It couldn't have worked out better for you, could it?' She found all at once that her eyes were full of tears, and brushed them angrily away. 'Well, you won't find everything's just as you want it after all. I'm not your prisoner any more – I owe you my life, perhaps, and for that I'm grateful. But that doesn't mean I intend to hand you my dowry on a plate for you to spend on your mistresses and your card games – if that's what you want then there are other women happy enough to give you that–' She pulled further away from him. 'I want to dismount.' It was not easy, but he did not hinder her – even helped her a little – and she found herself on the ground at his side looking up at him. Her voice was vibrant now with painful anger, and she plunged on, ignoring his attempt to break in.

'I despise you, and all you stand for. I knew nothing of courts and their ways, and fine noblemen, until I met you – and I wish to God it had stayed that way. They think nothing at court of bartering heart and soul for money, or position, or a kind word from the King. But I'm not like that. I thought you weren't either, but I know better now. Once I would gladly have given you everything I have, my life, my love, all I possess, for ever and ever – but for that I'd want more than you can ever give in return – not birth or position or wealth, but the things you don't even begin to understand – a loving heart, and loyalty, and faithfulness. Go back to your greedy, grasping court, and be happy if you can. I'll find my own way home.' And she turned then and ran away from him towards the little gate in the wall. She heard him call her name, and knew he was urging his horse after her, but she simply shouted furiously: 'Go away– Get out of my life!' And then she was through the gate, slamming it and bolting it behind her, and then, running, running half blinded with tears along the straight gravelled paths of the formal gardens towards the sleeping château.

Everyone was very kind to Kate. They seemed to understand that in her distraught, near-hysterical state no explanation of her absence was possible. She was put to bed with a hot brick at her feet, and dosed with spiced wine laced with laudanum, and left alone to sleep through what remained of the night and most of the next day.

She awoke at evening feeling heavy-eyed and depressed, but in full control of herself once more. Harry came with her supper, and a tender concern which surprised and touched her.

'The Queen doesn't expect you back at your duties until tomorrow, and not then unless you're up to it,' he reassured her, sitting down heavily on the edge of the bed. He took her hand in his and patted it gently. 'It didn't turn out as you'd hoped then.'

Clearly he wanted some explanation, and Kate supposed she owed him one; but it was not easy to know where to begin. All he knew, after all, was that a mysterious message had come last night saying that she had run away with Tristan de Plouvinel.

'The message was untrue, all of it,' Kate told him at last. 'I… It's a long story … I don't think I can tell you everything now.

But someone took me prisoner – I think they were going to kill me – and then I ... escaped.'

Harry smiled ruefully.

'Make a habit of that sort of thing, don't you? Time you gave it up and settled down to a nice quiet life. Don't you think so?' Kate nodded, smiling too, though a little tremulously. Then Harry asked: 'All that about the Comte de Plouvinel – it was all a pack of lies, was it? He had nothing to do with it?'

Kate hesitated. 'Not really,' she said. 'Only–'

'Only what?'

'Nothing.'

'Hm,' said Harry, observing her closely. 'It's just that when the message came the Queen said to me that she thought you'd lost your heart to someone, and it looked as though that was who it was. Seemed to make sense at the time – explained a lot of things. But you say it was all invention?'

'That part of it, yes,' she said cautiously.

'Just as well,' commented Harry, relaxing. 'Not the man for you to tangle with – most unlikely to have honourable intentions towards a girl like you. What with his birth, and wealth, and so on–'

'But he's giving up going to sea– They say

287

he needs a rich wife–'

Harry chuckled.

'You're hardly that, are you?'

'What about my dowry?' demanded Kate, with a hint of indignation. This time Harry laughed outright, openly derisive.

'What good do you think that would do him? Wouldn't last five minutes at court. Besides, he's rich as Croesus – made enough at sea to keep him ten times over as extravagantly as he could wish. He can marry where he pleases – but he'll go for good birth, you can be sure of that – one of the old noble families like himself. Always do, these French noblemen, if they can afford to.' He paused, his gaze suddenly intent. 'Kate, you didn't think–? You didn't really think he might–?'

Kate found herself colouring deeply. She didn't want to answer him, because if she did so then she would have to face the full implications of what he said, and she was afraid of what she might find there. After a little while she said unsteadily: 'The Marquise de Tacoignières said he needed a rich wife.'

Harry looked startled.

'Did she indeed? What was she playing at, I wonder? Warning you off maybe – could that be it?'

It was only too likely, but Kate averted her gaze and said nothing. Sensitive to her reluctance, Harry patted her hand again. 'Still, never mind! You can tell me the rest when you feel like it. Eat your supper now before it gets cold.'

Kate ate, but without enthusiasm, and a short time later, realising she wanted to be alone, Harry left her, urging her to rest a little more.

But there was no likelihood at all that she would rest. She got out of bed and paced the room, now and then pausing at the window, or flinging herself restlessly into a chair.

What had she done?

So many things came back to her now. There was that flicker of surprise on Tristan's face when Hervé spoke of her broken engagement. That had told her that until then Tristan had not known of it. And if he had thought her still betrothed, waiting perhaps only for a convenient moment to return to Ireland and be married, then would he have thought of marrying her? And if he did not wish to marry her, why should he risk his life to save her, unless he cared for her? Whatever had brought him there – even if it was just a liking of adventure – she was certain now that a wish to lay

289

hands on her dowry did not enter into it.

In any case, she wondered, did he even know of the existence of her dowry? Very likely he did, for Aunt Tabby might well have told him when he questioned her. But it did not matter, for Harry had shown her how small and insignificant it would seem to him. If it had not been for Marguerite and Hervé together, it would not have occurred to her to think that her little fortune might interest Tristan de Plouvinel.

Marguerite had planted the seeds of doubt in Kate's mind. She had intervened when Tristan seemed to be showing some kind of interest in Kate. She had employed Hervé to use Kate as a decoy to lure Tristan to his death, a scheme which had almost been successful. It was clear enough that she wanted Tristan for herself, and was determined that if she could not have him then no one else should either. But did she know for certain what Kate had only now begun to guess? Had she tried to prevent Kate, even at the point of death, from finding out the truth?

For Tristan had asked her to marry him. And if he did not need her dowry then there was only one possible reason for that proposal: love. Love that made him indifferent to her poverty and her lack of birth and her

English blood. Love such as she had hardly even dared to hope he would ever feel.

And she, blind foolish headstrong Kate, had thrown all that in his face and run from him, and thus in a moment of madness destroyed all the wonderful possibilities that he had, against all the odds, held out to her.

Bitterly regretful, Kate turned her anger on herself, weeping and raging and wishing with everything she had that she could unlive the past hours, and go back to that moment outside the garden and make it all different somehow. Her tortured mind imagined how it might have been if she had waited, and asked, and listened. Would she have heard then the loving words she had only ever dreamed of hearing? Would she by now be Tristan's wife, looking forward to a life shared with him?

She flung herself face down on the bed, her fists drumming on the pillow, and sobbed piteously for all she had thrown away.

She had little rest that night. She had in any case slept too long through the day to be able easily to sleep again. But she knew that even if she had been tired she would not have slept. Her anger turned very soon to despair, for she could see no way of redeeming her own foolishness. She could hardly go now to Tristan and say: 'I was mistaken after all. I should like to marry you' – not after all the terrible things she had said to him, her refusal to listen, her complete misjudgement of the situation. 'If I were a proud man like Tristan,' she thought, 'and someone had spoken to me like that, I don't think I should ever be able to forgive her, whatever I'd felt before. I certainly wouldn't want to marry her any more.' Which left her with no alternative but to go and take up her post in the Auvergne, and try and learn to live with the horrible knowledge that she had wilfully ruined her own life. It was a bitter reflection to carry with her through the long lonely hours of the night.

It might have been easier if there had been some occasional sound to break the stillness. But it seemed that in all that overcrowded building she was the only one awake. Not even a mouse scuttled his way through the quiet passages, and if owls called in the garden or the forest she did not hear them. All that she heard were the echoing phrases in her head which fed her bitterness and her regret. 'Hervé was right: I wish to marry you ... and of course a rich marriage is essential... She didn't know you were after her dowry.' Poisonous phrases all,

that had fuelled that terrible misunder-
standing, and turned to nothing all the
memories which might have told her the
truth. That embrace at St Malo, so passionate that the thought of it could still set
her trembling; the talk and laughter, the
hours spent lingering at the supper table;
Tristan turning to her in the coach coming
here, and saying approvingly: 'A clear head
and a warm heart – it is a good combination
you have, English Miss Kate.' But it was
more of a torment to remember Tristan's
tenderness, the delight of his company, the
way he said her name, than to think of the
steps which had led her to miss all the signs
which should have told her what he felt. She
lay in her narrow bed thinking of him, longing achingly to feel his arms about her, to be
near him, to hear him say that he loved her;
and knowing that what once might have
been hers now was lost to her for ever.

At last, just for a little while, she slid into
the merciful forgetfulness of sleep. Only to
be woken just a short time later by some
sound which for a moment she could not
place. She sat up in bed, listening hard.

The sound came again, clear and distinct,
from somewhere beyond the window. Its
resonance suggested it came from the court-

yard, echoing about the high enclosing walls. It was a kind of scraping wail, familiar and yet somehow wrong. She could not place it, and lay straining her ears in case it was repeated.

It was: and this time doubled or trebled, in a layered mingling of varied pitch and intensity, astonishingly loud. And she realised that she had not recognised it simply because it should not have been there at all. It was, clearly and unmistakably, the sound of someone – several people – tuning a number of stringed instruments.

But how was that likely, or even possible, in the darkened courtyard of a château in the middle of the night? Fascinated curiosity pushed Kate's misery to the back of her mind. She slid from the bed and pattered barefoot over the cold floor, and opened the window. Here and there about the courtyard others had done the same, and in one or two windows a candle gleamed, kindly illuminating a night-capped head, or outlining a dark silhouette.

The sounds ceased, and there was an interval of expectant silence, broken only by the sharp barking of a disturbed dog. The next moment the instruments sprang into united and orderly life, and a lilting languishing lovesick melody floated entrancingly into the frosty night air. The dog began to howl.

Smiling to herself, Kate pushed the window wide and crept forward on to the balcony, crouching down so that she could see without being seen. There were four players grouped on the gravel path which bordered the little garden at a point just below her room. They sat, incongruously, on ornate chairs which must have been brought with admirable stealth from indoors. A fifth man stood beside them, a torch held high in his hand, the red-gold glow illuminating the little space around them. There was a sixth, too, Kate realised after a moment, lurking almost out of sight in the shadow beyond the reach of the torchlight, a tall black figure, very still and silent. Something about his motionless watchful presence held her gaze, but it was too dark for her to make out any detail of his appearance. And by now the musicians were facing problems of distracting magnitude.

They played on with stern determination, ruthlessly accurate in note and tempo, and every sweet melancholy phrase was underlined with doleful vigour by the dog. They struggled on, rage and frustration growing with each moment, until at last, tried beyond endurance, one of them gave a staccato command, and the playing ceased.

The dog fell silent. A sigh of relief was almost audible from the disturbed sleepers about the courtyard. One candle went out, and a window slammed shut.

A conference pianissimo, was being conducted below, with considerable heat, if the expressions and gestures were any guide. Three of the musicians were now on their feet; a chair fell over, unnoticed; and the tall figure emerged from the shadows, vigorously gesticulating. It was, unmistakably, Tristan de Plouvinel.

Kate stared, wide-eyed, her breath drawn sharply in and held in disbelief. What on earth was he doing here at this time of night with a string quartet and a torchbearer for company?

The conference was abruptly broken off, with agreement evidently, for Tristan retreated again into the shadows, the chair was restored to its place, the violinist gave a wave of his bow, and the music recommenced. So, with wholehearted abandon, did the dog. And then, as if to add his weight to the uneven conflict, the torchbearer began to sing in a high and piercing counter-tenor.

A window shot open opposite and a

furious male voice roared for silence. The dog howled more loudly than ever. The clear notes of the counter-tenor reached undreamed-of heights. And there was an audible twang. The playing ceased abruptly, tailing off in the fluent cursing of the violinist with the broken string. The counter-tenor came to a tremulous and uncertain halt. The dog continued to howl.

All patience gone, the violinist jumped to his feet and waved his instrument in the air and unleashed a stream of furious vituperation in the direction of the dog. A second dog began to bark. The other musicians started to argue, beyond caring any longer about the noise they made. Tristan strode forward, his furious voice pleading for order and peace and music.

By now the whole château was awake, brilliantly illuminated and buzzing with commotion. On the crowded balconies the angry voices multiplied minute by minute, and the jeering, ribald cries. Someone, seizing his moment with care, upturned a chamber-pot full on the head of the furious counter-tenor. It extinguished his torch, but did nothing to still the extraordinary din. It was worse now, for the two noisy dogs had roused the entire population of the royal hunting kennels, and an incredible frenzy of barking underlined the deafening human cacophony below.

Kate, utterly fascinated, leaned up on the balustrade and watched, and laughed and laughed as she had not laughed for a very long time, until the tears came and her sides ached and she could laugh no more.

Tristan saw her. He stepped clear of the shouting musicians and stood looking up at her, with an expression of anguish on his face such as she had never seen there before. He spread his arms, gesturing help-lessly, and his lips moved, but there was not a hope that she could make out a word he said. She shook her head, trying to suppress the wild laughter which was shaking her still. Tristan drew breath and tried again, shouting with all the despairing power he could muster in a voice which reverberated about the courtyard and came clear and unmistakable to her ears.

'It was for you, Kate – for you, to tell you that I love you!'

Kate stood quite still, the smile struck from her face, slowly allowing his meaning to reach her and spread its warmth and delight to every part of her. And the laughter leapt up in her again, and she pulled herself on to the balustrade and sat there precariously balanced, bare feet dangling.

'Catch me!' she called. Tristan stood there, appalled.

'No! No, Miss Kate – it is too far– For the love of God–!'

It *was* rather a long way. Kate acknowledged his good sense, but it did not in any way quell her bubbling high spirits. She cried: 'Wait there!' and ran without thinking just as she was, dressed in nothing but her shift, out of her room and down the nearby stairs that brought her to the courtyard. She was too happy to care how cold it was. She ran through the echoing yard to where Tristan stood, silent and apart from the chaos about him, his face stern with anxiety, and took his hands in hers, swinging them gently.

'Oh Tristan – Tristan – I've never seen anything like it in my life!'

He stood looking down into her face, frowning, his gravity unshaken, almost disapproving.

'It was for you – do you understand, it was for you! How it was, I do not know, but you did not believe I loved you – so I planned a serenade, like a romance – the very best musicians. But you see how it is–!' His hands gestured with despair. Kate's eyes travelled to the riotous scene beyond him, and she giggled helplessly.

'Tristan, it's wonderful – don't you see – perfect! I shall never forget–' Then she caught sight of the appeal in his eyes, and relented. She raised her voice higher still to make sure he heard, but her tone was penitent. 'Can you forgive me for what I said last night? I can't think what made me – I should have known – it was stupid to think you could even be interested in my little dowry–'

His hands held her arms, and his expression lightened a little. He pulled her under the shelter of the balcony, where the noise was fractionally less. 'I do not know how you could think that for one moment – but perhaps I did not enough show you what I felt for you– That is why–' One hand indicated the chaotic yard, and he left the sentence unfinished, saying instead, 'But if you know the truth, I am glad. I am not in need of a rich wife, you know, and I never was. I have enough and to spare for myself, and my wife, and all my needs as long as I live.'

'Even if you give up going to sea?'

'I have already given up. The *Marguerite* is sold. There is a place still for the corsairs, even in peace time, but I shall not be among them. My wandering days are over. But not, little Miss Kate, because I wish to waste my time at court. I shall go home, to my estates, and make you hold your breath in admiration at my excellent management. And you, most loved Kate, will share with me all that I do. We shall live and work together, side by side, you and I, and the children – our children–'

They had not heard the sudden stir of new excitement through the courtyard, nor even the almost instant stillness which followed it, only the dogs still protesting. They did not know that King James himself had emerged on to the balcony, determined at last to quell the inexplicable commotion which had disturbed his rest. It was not until Tristan's final words carried with total clarity across the now silent yard that they both realised with horror that the entire population of the château must have heard every word.

Their eyes met in dismay, and then they turned very slowly, and looked across at the astonished face of the exiled monarch. Tristan, red-faced, bowed. Kate, curtseying, was aware with renewed hilarity of all the eyes watching them with breathless curiosity. She thought that the King too looked as if laughter was not far from the surface.

Then he acknowledged their deference with a brief nod of the head, swept a final glance over the chastened throng on all sides, and went back to bed. There was a momentary pause, as of relief at a punishment deferred, and then one by one the courtiers left the balconies, the musicians gathered up their instruments, the servants emerged to remove the chairs and tidy up the debris. Kate watched as Tristan paid off the musicians and thanked them gravely, and then turned back to her and stood looking down at her, his hands holding hers. And this time he too was laughing.

'Oh, *chérie,* but you are my delight! And I want so much that you should be happy always–'

She reached out to him as he drew her into his arms and folded them close about her, shutting out the world. His mouth came down to meet hers, and she ran her fingers into the thickness of his hair, and gave herself up to his embrace without fear or doubt or hesitation. They were together at last, and nothing now could part them, for they belonged to each other, for always. And Kate knew as joy filled her to overflowing that everything lay before them still, for this was only the beginning.

The publishers hope that this book has given you enjoyable reading. Large Print Books are especially designed to be as easy to see and hold as possible. If you wish a complete list of our books please ask at your local library or write directly to:

Dales Large Print Books
Magna House, Long Preston,
Skipton, North Yorkshire.
BD23 4ND

This Large Print Book, for people
who cannot read normal print,
is published under the auspices of

THE ULVERSCROFT FOUNDATION

... we hope you have enjoyed this book.
Please think for a moment about those
who have worse eyesight than you ...
and are unable to even read or enjoy
Large Print without great difficulty.

You can help them by sending a
donation, large or small, to:

**The Ulverscroft Foundation,
1, The Green, Bradgate Road,
Anstey, Leicestershire, LE7 7FU,
England.**
or request a copy of our brochure for
more details.

The Foundation will use all donations
to assist those people who are visually
impaired and need special attention
with medical research, diagnosis
and treatment.

Thank you very much for your help.